MEMORY
of
LIGHT

MEMORY *of* LIGHT

RUTH VANITA

PENGUIN
VIKING
An imprint of Penguin Random House

VIKING

USA | Canada | UK | Ireland | Australia
New Zealand | India | South Africa | China

Viking is part of the Penguin Random House group of companies
whose addresses can be found at global.penguinrandomhouse.com

Published by Penguin Random House India Pvt. Ltd
7th Floor, Infinity Tower C, DLF Cyber City,
Gurgaon 122 002, Haryana, India

First published in Viking by Penguin Random House India 2020

10 9 8 7 6 5 4 3 2 1

ISBN 9780670093519

Typeset in Adobe Caslon Pro by Manipal Technologies Limited, Manipal
Printed at Thomson Press India Ltd, New Delhi

www.penguin.co.in

for Sujata Raghubir

न हि विचलति मैत्री दूरतु अपि स्थितानम्

1

I absorb every word she says, leaning in slightly, a snake following the piper's swaying head. She's in my sister's room—is it now mine? Light slants in from the terrace, and I hear my mother moving about outside.

A little restless, a little sad, back from one of her journeys, she talks to me. I take her hand and stroke it lightly. If two lines of lightning touch the same spot on earth do they merge or fizzle out?

My eyes stir. Still here, after all. Past and present stone walls, future a window of air. Between us now, Chapla, is the fourth wall, a wall of light, without windows. Dreaming, I pass through it. I close my eyes, hoping to return to the place where I was a moment ago, but the wall refuses to melt . . .

Anyone can interrupt my writing, and everyone does. Nadira pokes her head through the curtains. 'Come with me to Ram Awadh Johri? I have to order a necklace for Bhajju's wedding and also pick up that locket you gave me. I'd better do it before he gives it to someone else the way he did my ring; luckily, it was Bakhshi he gave it to, and she recognized it.'

'He's been seeing you two together for years,' I say, covering up my papers and standing up to stretch. 'He probably knew she would give it to you.'

'No, he often gives things to the wrong people these days; he's beginning to lose his memory with age. I don't think I should wait for him to send it.'

'I told you not to leave your jewellery with him. Why don't you give him just the small jobs that he can do in your presence, and give the important stuff to that clever son of his who's fought with him and set up his own shop?'

'What? How cruel that would be—after the years and years that he's done all our work. So what if he's losing his memory—none of us is growing any younger. And I don't like that son of his—he thinks he's descended from heaven just because his name is Hanuman and he's built a big house and painted it an ugly blue. I'd rather Ram Awadh lose my stuff than Hanuman find it.'

'Very good—then don't complain, pigeon. May he lose many more of your things to make you happy. I'll be down in a minute.' I pinch her plump, comfortable cheek on my way up to the roof.

In the late afternoon warmth, the winged ones surround me, whirring. Sleepy winter sunshine in an unusually quiet moment—the girls are dozing away last evening's pleasures, work, quarrels, the night's fatigue. Frail clouds, sky almost indigo deep. Beyond our neighbourhood stretches the city, white, gleaming, with touches of pink, trees like bunchy green flowers between the buildings.

Guddu settles on my shoulder and nibbles the top of my ear. She's ageing, her rose-brown face starting to lose its lustre. Feathered beings should not age. Like *pari*, fairies, they should appear, disappear, but stay forever young. Like young poets, young dancers I remember, who melted, radiant, ice on a summer afternoon. Not slowly into a puddle like the rest of us. I try to run lightly down the steps as I used to, but my knees refuse.

I lift the curtain at my mother's door to see if she wants us to bring her anything. She's reading the life of a saint and looks up querulously. 'No, what do I need? Sitting here alone all the time.'

'Alone, alone!' Mitthu chimes in, head on one side, as if to point out how often he hears this word. Reproachful eyes, black, beady, fixed on me, he pushes a half-eaten green chili towards the bars. I wish I could smack him, but I bite my lip, take the cage out and hang it in the gallery so that he can see the sky. Taking a deep breath, I look back in.

'Eat on time, don't wait for us, Ammi. I'll tell Shabbo.'

'*Arey*, that girl has no sense of time. She's too busy adorning herself and expecting admirers to come to the kitchen door.'

'Really?'

'Of course. You're so taken up with your scribbling you don't notice. Why do you think that errand boy from Sandela—what's his name with the big earrings . . .?'

'Mangu?'

'Yes, Mangat Ram—why do you think he's always standing at the back door calling for water to drink? So that she'll bring it out, what else?'

'Oh, Ammi, it's winter's end, one gets thirsty. And water from inside is colder than water kept outside.'

Ammi sniffs and returns to her reading.

She was once the best performer in the city, I remind myself, pushing down the black fog that rises in my chest. Only mothers and sisters, or those who become like mothers or sisters, can irritate one in this precisely disproportionate way. She once had scores of men at her feet—our own noblemen, courtiers, magnates, and also the English officers with their presents of jewels, money, clothes—she still has those French shoes from Herbert Sahib—no wonder she feels neglected now.

Neither of her two daughters inherited her gift. My sister Shirin sings—or sang—adequately. More important, she knows how to get what she wants. That's how she became Nawab Ghaziuddin's umpteenth wife. I was considered too clumsy to dance, my voice, though pleasant, had no staying power, and worst of all, I generally thought of a witty response after the moment had passed. Nor was I beautiful; my looks were just good enough to make one wish for more. Starting to read at the age of three was not much use, it turned out. I scribble passable verse, but that is not a particularly valuable skill because there are poets in every lane and alley, and several great ones. Then again, Sharad says, many who are thought great now won't be remembered in fifty years, let alone a hundred.

Ammi is from Shahjahanabad, the hub of the world. She never tires of listing the noblemen who gathered at her grandmother's home in Delhi. She names their wives too, at whose homes her young mother sometimes performed. I notice her listeners sighing inwardly when she repeats these stories, and sometimes I try to change the subject. Nani was so fair, Ammi says, that her skin was transparent. When she drank, you could see the water flow down her throat. I grow more and more embarrassed because Ammi herself is dark and has never been considered beautiful, and all this leads up to her hinting that her own father was none other than the Emperor himself, the Mughal lord of the world, actually lord of not much more than Delhi. If he was, it was of little use to you, I sometimes feel like snapping, because you had to run away to Banaras when that cruel traitor who called himself Imad-ul Mulk blinded the Emperor and his mother. She was one of us, his mother, a dancer before she became a queen, and they say she had an affair with a *khwajasarai*. She'd have been better off remaining one of us—she'd have kept her eyes.

I go down the next flight of stairs. Despite my annoyance with Ammi's complaints I check on Shabbo who turns out to be industriously grinding mint chatni just outside the kitchen, keeping one eye on the crowd of children in the yard and one on a simmering pot. Winter sunlight filters through a haze of smoke from the *chulha*. Why is it still smoking so late in the day? Oddly, I like the smell of smoke on a declining winter afternoon, a time of day Chapla used to find depressing. In the back alley, an urchin is riding a street dog he's trying to adopt against his mother's wishes. The women above leading the life of art, the men and the workers below, their life spilling out on to the streets. I hear the girls upstairs practising, the steady hum of the tanpura, feet stamping, ankle bells ringing.

In the gallery, Mahtab Baji is painting her nails, applying each tiny stroke just as meticulously as when her hands were unwrinkled. To tell the truth, they are still remarkably smooth for her age. I ask if she wants anything. 'Yes, Nafis,' she says in her slow, creamy voice, a bit like a contented purr, 'Please get me some *imartis*. I don't know why but since yesterday I've been longing for them. I was going to send Shabbo but I haven't been able to get hold of her.' Shabbo, hidden by the gallery's overhang, pretends not to hear and I smile to myself; Mahtab Baji daintily consumes large quantities of sweets yet manages to stay sleek and milk-white while I, trying to control what I eat, break out in spots and put on weight.

Mangu bows as I emerge from the front door and get into the palanquin. I give him a note for Sharad. What huge dark eyes the boy has, and what long lashes. We're not going far but the streets are crowded and the palanquin bearers are bored so we have to devise work for them.

Nadira, waiting in the palanquin, is counting coins she extracts from her bodice pocket. As she concentrates, her tongue flicks each corner of her mouth and her forehead twitches, movements I've seen almost every day for years, the same yet different as her face ages.

We pass Roshan-ud Daula's sweetshop, always obscured by a crowd, some devouring hot sweets, others shouting their orders over many heads. The present-day Roshan, imperturbable as his father and grandfather, proceeds with his work, unmoved by the hubbub. The faces have changed, the shop is bigger, but the scene is the same. Familiarity, one of the small consolations of ageing, I think, but don't say. Such sententious thoughts are best kept to oneself. I hope Sharad, retired to his childhood village, finds such markers there, and has stopped missing the ones accumulated here.

Food is another consolation, to my mind. While Nadira argues with the jeweller (she's a skilful bargainer, which he enjoys; I, on the other hand, am no fun for him), I pick up *nankhatai* from the Surati Bania three shops down. Madanmohan is coming to see me tonight, and he has the oddest taste in snacks to accompany his drinks. He wants the actual sweetmeat, not a sweet young thing. I don't see him much since he moved to Faizabad, so it's a special occasion.

On the way back, I listen with half an ear to Nadira's repetitive worries about her granddaughter Sona. 'Such a dreamer she is—doesn't want to read or write or dance or sing. All she wants to do is run around or lie on the swing, gazing at the sky, or play with the deer and the pigeons. She's behaving like a good-for-nothing boy. We may as well have had a boy.' Nadira can't believe that her precious heir, her only daughter Azzo's only daughter Sona may not turn out to be a star. We have other potential stars, I could remind her. But that usually upsets her even more so I refrain.

The sun is setting when we get back. As my foot touches the ground I realize I've forgotten the imratis—how annoying—I was right next-door to the shop, and was even thinking about how it hasn't changed much. Dreamers and grandmothers of dreamers! Mangu is back, and Sharad has actually written a note. He doesn't always reply right away. It depends on his mood. I go up to the roof and read it, in the hush of the pigeons' flutterings as they prepare to roost and the tumult of birds wheeling in great circles and ovals above, before they settle, twittering, in the trees that flow down to the rooftops. A line of screaming green cuts through the circles, parrots on their way to rest. Nothing much in the letter—the usual little goings-on. The new breed of tomatoes he's growing, his niece's marriage, his back pain. This niece was his housekeeper, but a younger one is going to take her place. He may come to the city to consult the surgeon at the Residency who also attends on the Nawab. He'll hear the new singers at the impending ceremony—one of our girls, Bhajju, already under prince Nasiruddin's protection, is going to become his next wife. And visit his friends at court. And see me. I look up and across the rooftop; I've always liked the way my shadow makes me look in the evening—tall and slender instead of short and inclined to dumpiness.

A pinprick in my heart as I roll up the note to put in my basket full of many such little rolls. A nudge, like the ache in my knees as I descend the rickety stairs. I must remember to have them repaired. Shabbo hasn't yet lit the lamp in my room. When I call, she yells back something unintelligible and I hear her anklets jingling as she takes off in the opposite direction. Perhaps there's something to Ammi's complaints. My nurse, Dadda, comes in, muttering, and lights the lamp, the tremor in her hands endangering the cushions. Hard to recall her as that sprightly busybody running in and out with her little girl at her heels.

By the time I hear Madan's voice downstairs, the lamp has found its tempo, and down the gallery Nadira's daughter and granddaughter are singing, their voices rising and falling as if with the flame. An unusual lot they seem to me, my men friends. Or perhaps I'm the unusual one, having refused a patron, refused to travel, refused childbirth. And embraced instead these interrupted conversations, scribblings, memories.

Madan, Sharad, the poet Insha—I saw each one for the first time by lamplight. That's not unusual, because it's at the lamp-lighting hour that men visit us, after the day's work, to shake off money-counting, the stratagems of court and business, the demands and schemings of parents, siblings, wives, children, aunts, uncles. To live briefly in the eternal youth of conversation, poetry, music, dance. In the shadows thrown by lamps, wayward, whimsical, almost anyone seems alluring—at least for a while. We sleep much of the day but how do the men continue their daily routines after staying awake most of the night? I suppose they manage because they don't visit us every night.

It was in Mir Insha's entourage that I met Sharad. Cool as his name, the son of a trader in cloth whose wealth tripled, then quadrupled when fabrics from Kalkatta and Dhaka poured into the market during those years before and after the drought when the city kept growing, sprouting markets, shops, inns. Enough to allow Sharad to pursue his interest in designing and decorating homes and palaces. There was a restraint to Sharad that coexisted with a peacock-like awareness of his looks. A taut discipline held in balance those gazelle eyes, arched brows, flowing locks. When I first met him, Sharad was one of Mir Insha's few students, in his shadow. Then they drifted apart as so many do, sooner or later.

Madan is about as different from both of them as it's possible to be—a tradesman with a tradesman's canniness that manages to be quick and obtuse at the same time. Him I first saw hesitantly entering Ammi's room with a group of businessmen. A bit like a turtle slowly venturing out of its shell.

Here he is now, and he's lost some weight, I notice, but still has a paunch. He tells Dadda there's a sack of rice and a bunch of sugarcane downstairs, and she summons the boys to carry them to the storeroom. Mitthu announces Madan's arrival with a cackle, and Madan stops to feed him a shred of the sugarcane that he's brought up for him. I've always preferred the pigeons' cooing to the parrots' gabble so I draw the curtain across my doorway and call out to Shabbo to put the cage inside and cover it for the night. That will silence Mitthu. Not for the first time I wish I could release him to join his tribe in the sky but I can't because they would tear him to bits.

'Where's that piece of your heart?' Madan teases, as he settles into the cushions with a sigh.

'Nadira? She's gone to the palace; Shirin is having a session for the *lal pari*. Nadira is much nicer than I am; thank God she keeps up with everyone so I don't have to.'

'Ah, she's a lucky one—that Nadira Bai. Well, I'm happy she's out so I get some time alone with my girl.' He's joking, of course—odd that it's pleasant to have once been desired, even by someone for whom desire never so much as flickered. 'By the way, how's Shirin's feud with the other begams going?'

'No idea. Perhaps that's why she's summoning the red fairy—to defeat the others and become chief among the junior wives. But there's no way she can win that battle.' I find the ups and downs of my sister's marriage to the Nawab and her rivalries with his wives exhausting, not least because my mother gets so animated talking about them. Wives by courtesy; only the first four are really married to him.

'Speaking of which, have you heard that the prince's next big marriage may be to a *firangin*? They call her Vilayati Begam. She looks something like the one your Chapla Bai may have had a bit of a crush on. What was her name—the one you met at Martin Sahib's house?'

My body seems to constrict, a trick it has when that name is spoken. But I respond calmly, as I have for so many years.

'The wife of Plowden Sahib. Her name was Sufia but Chapla called her Lizbeth. I don't think it meant anything, though. Some people just have a flirtatious manner; it's part of their charm. Or perhaps that's what charm is.'

'No, charm is the art of listening. Chapla Bai was perfect at that. She would get everything out of you, and hardly tell you anything, but ever after you would feel as if you were one of her intimates. You're not so bad at weaving that sort of spell yourself, my dear.'

'She's certainly cast a spell on Kashi.' I hand him the platter with the nankhatai and nuts, and start making *paan*.

'Yes, quite the reigning queen. I hear whoever she promotes has it made. But no daughters or granddaughters?'

'No, just a son.'

'That's a pity. No one to inherit all those gifts.'

'Well, our Azzo—Nadira's daughter, you know—spent a couple of years with her in Kashi and learnt a lot.' Madan doesn't visit often now, and I'm not sure how many details he remembers.

'Of course, of course.' He chuckles. 'And acquired her own daughter there. Don't tell Nadira Bai I said this but her daughter Azizan is not a patch on her sister, the first Azizan.'

'*Chhath*, you always had strange tastes.' He gives me a look, and I giggle. 'Also, things we remember from when we were young shine brighter. I think our Azzo is more attractive.'

'Where did the first Azizan come from, by the way?'

'Kashmir. That's why she was so fair. Nadira's mother picked her up in Meerut, and she turned out very well.' I keep to myself my less complimentary thoughts about the first Azizan.

'She really was from Kashmir? I know the foreign sahibs thought any of you who sang Kashmiri songs were from Kashmir.'

'Yes, but she really was.' White as a ghost, standing at my door, holding the curtain back, asking question after question. Madan continues with his.

'Did your Azzo go to Kashi this year as well?'

'Briefly, at Holi. She danced with them at Burhwa Mangal.'

'Ah, Burhwa Mangal at Kashi—I remember it, and it certainly does shine brighter. The illuminations, the girls, the boys, each more fairy-faced than the next! And the way those barges are decorated, like a string of palaces. The end of Holi and the start of the fierce season.'

'I like Dhulendi, the way everything seems faintly golden or rose-coloured, depending on the light.'

'Yes, I didn't mind the dust and powder then. Today I'd go a long way to avoid it. My breathing problems, you know. When did you last see her?'

'At Basant. She brought her girls to the palace here.'

'Is she happy?'

'I suppose. Older, calmer—aren't we all? Rupa is a sweet girl.' Why do I think of us as girls and boys though we're now grandparents?

'Rupa? Wasn't she called Champa?'

'That was a long time ago. She's been with Rupa for fifteen years.'

He returns to his earlier idea. 'Chapla's a princess of sorts too—isn't she the daughter of—which Raja of Kashi was it?'

'Chait Singh, the one who started the Burhwa Mangal fair. So they say.' What does it matter, though, who her father was? She's her mother's daughter and always was. Madan is still talking.

'Raja Chait Singh—yes, what a racket he raised—when was it? Years and years ago. Lord, how old I am! When he revolted against the Company Bahadur and brought his forces all the way here. You're too young to remember, but I happened to be at the Resident's house here on some business when his men appeared and almost stormed it.'

'He attacked Martin Sahib's house too, didn't he?' I vaguely remember people talking about this when I was a child.

'Some of his men did, and that's why Martin Sahib built that moat around it.'

'At Lakh Pera? Was that the reason he built the moat? I thought he was trying to recreate a castle from his home in France, with a hundred thousand trees around it. Chapla and I saw pictures when we were at Lakh Pera, pictures of French castles with moats and turrets and drawbridges, and clouds in cold blue skies. I wish Nawab Sahib hadn't removed the moat. I liked it.'

Madan looks puzzled as well he may; he can't see the pictures rising in me—moat, river and sky, house floating between them, trees behind, dark layer on dark layer, the bridge that drew us in and folded up after us—and you, made of light.

'Well, as long as all of them leave us alone.' He smiles and takes my hand as I refill his glass.

'You still don't drink wine?'

'I don't.'

'What kind of life is this, without pleasure? And your life's work is supposed to be creating pleasure.'

The wine of life I drained all at once, now I drink milk and water. To distract him, I ask, 'More nankhatai?'

'Yes, it's very good.'

'Don't your wives make it at home?'

'They do, but sometimes one wants sweets from the bazaar.' He gives me an impish smile, then returns to Chapla.

'Chapla was a lot younger than you, no?'

'Five, nearly six, years.'

'That's a big difference. She was a child when you could have had one. Anyway, the whole thing was unlikely—it was as if I should want to marry the Nawab's daughter.'

'So you think we were completely mismatched?'

'No, not at all. It could have lasted. But you shouldn't have let her return alone to Kashi that summer. You should have gone with her. She's not used to being alone, and she's the sort whom people won't leave alone either.'

I look down at the wine I'm pouring, so he doesn't see me flinch as if pricked by a needle lurking in a cloth. Nearly thirty years for someone to come up with an explanation perhaps simple enough to be true.

2

It was at a session for the red fairy that we met. Those sessions were not the rage then, as they are now, but they did occur from time to time. Some woman who had a question about the future or who was upset because of her sister, her girlfriend, her paramour or her pesky servants, or among the begams, her mother-in-law or sister-in-law, would decide to consult the jinns and paris. The ones made of light, they called them.

I've forgotten now what Mattan Apa's session was about—perhaps she wanted to know what the future held for Bakhshi, her prize performer, or perhaps she was just in the mood for a get-together. It was a year after Mir Insha moved here from Faizabad, and a year before the English King George's fiftieth birthday celebrations. Mir Insha had arranged for Ammi to take my sister Shirin to Faizabad to perform there so I had to go alone to Mattan Apa's house to represent all of us.

Mattan Apa's *kotha* was at the corner of our lane, and Nadira, just my age, grew up there, with her sister, Azizan, from Kashmir, whom her mother had adopted in Meerut.

Her mother, Khanam Jaan, that wonderful singer, whom the Englishmen unkindly called Taanee, which I've been told means Dark in their language, died young—when was it?—three years before Chapla first came to town, I think—yes, it was in the year of the great drought, the year the Nawab, helped by Raja Tikait Rai, Mirza Raza, and Jhao Lal, started his fabulous construction projects to give work to the poor. Between Mattan Apa and my mother there simmered a rivalry much like the rivalries between poets, background music to all our other dramas. When Mattan Apa died, many years later, Ammi's strength seemed to drain from her. Even her stories lost their edge.

Between Mattan Apa's house and ours was a small and unimportant kotha, long and narrow, whose roof we girls routinely crossed when we wanted to meet. But since this was a special occasion, I decided to take the more formal route down the front lane.

The evening's gathering had been cut short because my mother was away; still, it was late into the night by the time I went downstairs, and looked in on the sleeping children, their nursemaids snoring close by, their dogs snoozing at the threshold. The oldest nurse, who had nursed me and whom I call Dadda, had her daughter, Heera, my foster-sister, curled into her. Looking at them I felt sleepy and wished I could stay home, but I made myself get dressed, and looked into Ammi's room for a red shawl. Mitthu (the present Mitthu's nominal ancestor) stirred and muttered under his covers. He was to my left, I remembered later. A good journey, even if it was just down the lane.

Nadira was away, so I sat down in a corner with her somewhat older friend Bakhshi. Her name is Murad Bakhsh but everyone calls her Bakhshi. Her extraordinary voice made their kotha the only real rival to ours after Nadira's mother died. But her reputation seemed not to affect her. She had an unruffled air and smelled cool even in the midst of such feverish affairs. The guests had gone to considerable lengths to dress in red from head to toe, and were asking all kinds of questions and working themselves up into a frenzy. I watched these performances with amusement.

'Don't you have anything to ask, Nafis *beti*?' Mattan Apa whispered loudly in my ear, her plump, sweaty shoulder pressing into mine. With the arrogance of the immune, I shook my head, thinking nothing would induce me to reveal my heart to a semi-literate woman who tossed her head around like a maddened pony, muttering and squealing while banging on a dholak. But that was before I had much to reveal or conceal.

After the questions had all been asked and answered more or less satisfactorily by—which jinn was it, Miyan Shah Dariya?—everyone sat around, talking, sipping wine. I was awake now, wishing I could get back to the poem I was working on, but reluctant to go out into the darkness from the scented warmth of the room. Mattan Apa had outdone herself reddening it up. Hung with crimson draperies, lit with scarlet-shaded candles that echoed the sapphire and ruby-tinted Persian carpet. The air itself seemed red, heavy with the scent of rose petals floating in copper bowls. Red wine, beetroot kababs, and red sweets made of carrots and pomegranate heaped on French china. Mattan Apa herself was in red satin.

Mattan Apa's friend, who had been possessed and whose name I forget, seemed to have recovered from her head-whirlings, and was handing out bits of her half-chewed paan to greedy, perspiring suppliants, their still-wet hair draped unpleasingly over their shoulders. Mattan Apa surveyed the room triumphantly.

A couple of pomegranate seeds popped in my mouth, filling it with an acrid, somewhat gritty sweetness. 'O Nafis, here's Ketaki Bai's daughter,' someone, I don't remember who, said. I looked up. She was half-smiling, half-laughing, in that semi-shy, semi-mischievous way to which I would become addicted.

Our eyes met, held. The room fell silent.

Stripped bare, I stood on the threshold of birth. Gazing into fire.

She was in white, all white against the redness. Was her hair open, as if freshly washed? Or is memory playing hide-and-seek with fantasy?

'Ammi didn't know you were coming. She's gone to Faizabad.'

'It was a last-minute thing. But I'll come again, I'm sure.' Still sunlight.

'*Arey*, Nafis, we've been talking about nothing else for at least two days.' Dulhan Jaan's voice glass crashing into a garden. 'Where have you been?' The others giggled.

'Nafis *bitiya* has better things to do; she's busy reading and writing,' Mattan Apa retorted. 'She takes all your gossip in one ear and lets it out the other.' There was a double edge to this reproach. Most of her girls were settled with patrons, unlike me, evidence of my indulgent mother's bad management.

If we said anything else, I don't remember what it was. Nor do I remember how I found myself in the silent lane, where the band seemed to be playing at one of Martin Sahib's parties as I looked at the sky through his big telescope and saw the stars up close. The darkness vibrated, as if I'd stared at the sun and then closed my eyes.

As if I had met again someone I'd known forever. In a former lifetime.

I'd known of her existence for the ever that is one's lifetime. Her mother, Ketaki Bai, then the star of Banaras, had performed with Mattan Apa and my mother at Nawab Sa'adat Ali Khan's wedding. The wedding was in Banaras and at least twenty groups performed there, but these three became sworn friends and exchanged *orhni*s. Mattan Apa was now so fat she had difficulty walking and could barely climb stairs, let alone dance, but she was supple once, no doubt. Ammi still has Ketaki Mausi's pink brocade orhni, beaded with pearls, ready to shred at a touch. I have no garment of Chapla's, just her poems and letters on paper soft and creased with age. And somewhere too that enameled ornament, the *dhukdhuki*. This one has a secret chamber that opens to reveal a fragment of paper with her name and mine joined in a couplet. Chapla was Ketaki Mausi's only daughter. She had a much younger brother.

All this history burnt up in a moment. I waved away the palanquin and walked home, light-headed though I had hardly touched the wine. Floating a foot above the ground, as I had done only in dreams, but dreams so vivid that for many years, floating seemed a memory of a common occurrence. Was the lane really silent as I remember it, dark buildings towering on both sides? If all the revellers had gone home, it must have been early morning.

Dawn. I stepped out on the gallery and breathed in like incense the woody scent from *chulhas* lined up along the back alley. There was the milkman's buffalo at our door; how patient and good she looked. And there was dear Heera going sleepily out to fill a pitcher with milk. The koyal repeated its two liquid notes. Air sang, and fragments of gold slanted down on a sheaf of rays. Like her gold-flecked eyes. Had such a glorious morning ever dawned before, and was any place as fortunate as our neighbourhood? Dadda came padding up with my buttermilk, and I squeezed her hard. She was startled but pleased.

'*Arey*, *arey*, what happened, bitiya?'

'Nothing.' It could only be told in song—how it felt to be alive on this particular morning.

I went in, her dusky voice running through me, and tried to scribble it into a song. I copied it out carefully and sent it over to Mattan Apa's. Not a poem about her; those came later. Just a playful riddle-verse about sunrise, and a note asking her to come over. My room seemed suddenly small and cramped, its windows looking down on the lane, its view blocked by the house opposite ours. Perhaps since I brought in the least profit or perhaps because I was the least demanding, my room was not as adorned as those of the other girls were. I did the best

I could, plumping up cushions, turning bolsters to hide their faded sides.

Instead of coming across the rooftops as we all did and as she would later, she rose up the stairway from the lane, in red this time, her head tilted a little to one side, her smiling face looking up at me.

She entered, hesitated, as if uncertain where to alight. Even before she sat down, she handed me a few pages of poetry in Brajbhasha, as if to ward off something, and said they were by her *gui'yaan*, someone called Champa. I thought the closeness of the names almost comical but of course didn't say so.

She also brought *parwal* sweets, their green outsides belying the creamy insides, slits encased in silver, each studded with an almond. 'Champa made them.'

Finally, we settled next to each other, the paan box between us, and talked, what about I don't recall. Late spring was speeding up into summer; the air crackled as if ready to leap into flame though the room was cool, dark, scented with *khus*. Her eyes.

I wanted to lean forward, put my lips to her cheek, and say, 'Why don't we drop these pretences?' Instead, I got up and crossed the room to call for *sharbat*.

Months later, she would tell me she had noticed the shape of my lips and my fingers that afternoon. She was leaving for Banaras next day.

Could I see her once more before then? At night, I slipped out of the mehfil, took my treasured collection of Abru's *ghazal*s, in which I had marked one with a feather, and crossed the rooftops. Not wanting to be seen, I stood outside her closed door for what seemed like an hour, and then left. Before dawn, I ventured out again. The pigeons complained when they heard me, and the cock let out an untimely crow.

Once more outside the door, whose lines and bolts I now seemed to know by heart. No sign, no sound. The sky was just beginning to brighten. I was turning to leave when the door opened. I thrust the book into her hands, muttered something and tried to flee. Bare throat, eyes mellow with sleep. She caught my arm, her low voice lower than usual. 'Wait. What . . .? How will I get it back to you?'

'You can bring it whenever you come back.' Someone was opening another door. I fled.

That's when the letter writing started. Sharad, generous as always, sent his family's letter carrier over at the merest hint that I could use him. Ammi was surprised when she returned a week later to find him coming to our door so often.

'So Ketaki's daughter really took to you, it seems.' She sighed. 'When I last saw her, she was a little imp. But I hear she now looks a lot like Ketaki at that age.'

'Much lovelier,' I wanted to say. I'd seen a portrait, Ketaki Mausi all in white, looking defiantly out at the world, an archway behind her. But I refrained, my usual bluntness tempered by a new awareness.

That was the summer of letters. Another river and other fields on its farther shore, places I've never seen yet seem to know. Kashi incandescent, a halo around her—lamplight, moonlight, the touch of dawn. Books she was reading, songs she was learning, people who are like characters in a romance; I've been hearing about them and asking after them for nearly thirty years yet some I've never seen and others met only briefly.

Between these descriptions she wrote that she wished I was there, walking down the ghats with her to the Ganga each morning before the day's practice or visiting the temple that Rani Ahalya Bai had rebuilt just a few years ago. A queen in the queen of cities.

'Last evening, I was walking home as the lamps were being lit. There's no light like lamplight reflected in Ganga-ji. You have to see her. Someone was singing the evening *arati*—O gracious one with lotus-eyes, lotus-face, lotus hands, red lotus feet, come, dwell in the lotus of my heart. It calmed me as I walked back, through the mist and smoke. No one but Gori had noticed I'd gone. She was waiting for me at our doorway. If you were here, would you have noticed? Would we sing together?' Gori was their small, brown cow; she was under-sized when born and was bullied by her twin, so Chapla had raised her by hand and now she followed her around like a chick following its mother.

'I'm reading the Kama Sutra with my teacher, and also the Puranas. I'll write out some parts for you. Send me bits of what you're reading and writing. I have to go and feed Kishen now. He's got a new trick this week—won't eat from anyone's hands but mine. You're very good at feeding people, aren't you? I felt as if I could spend several days just eating and sleeping in your room.'

As I sat, writing, reading, re-writing, re-reading, the papiha cried out his three notes, repeated, repeated,

repeated, shortening with the heightening intensity, rising to a crescendo and then abruptly stopping. He calls that way every summer, but that year he stationed himself on a tree just opposite my room and seemed to cry out for me alone.

Letters—all over the world, people are writing them to each other, and have been writing them for centuries. Surely they must repeat the same phrases. Sometimes I wonder if our faces are repeated too—how do I know that a hundred years ago there wasn't a girl who looked exactly like Chapla or that a hundred years from now there won't be another? Why am I so sure that these letters I now almost never look at are unique? That no one ever said just this in quite this way?

It felt like Banaras was next door because people from our lane went there so often, following the Nawabs who were always coming and going. When I read her letters I wanted to see the city where she had grown up.

~

All of us are living in a wooden house, shaped like a big boat. It's full of people, and the children are running, playing, shouting. Chapla and Rupa are visiting. Rupa and Nadira talk while I move around, getting things done. In fits and snatches, Chapla tells me about some trouble of hers. We want to sit and converse but we can't because there are so many others going in and out. The want keeps building as our hands touch briefly, as we exchange fragments, words. Finally, we go out to the back of the house and she lies down on a large, wooden swing seat. I sit near her and she talks at some length. We embrace briefly, I murmur something, and she says, I know, I know. Filled with bliss, I tell her to walk down to the sea. I point, she turns to look, and there is the quiet sea. On the shore, half submerged, is a large rock encrusted with shells and sea creatures. Kishen, Sona and the other children are clambering all over it. And near them I see a small, starved-looking lion. Afraid, I call them to come back in. They rush into the house, we follow, and the lion comes through the door too, but I chase it out.

I wake; as it ebbs out of me I recognize it—the old sensation of being slanted entirely towards her even as I go about the day's business. I can't recall it at will but somewhere it slumbers intact.

~

A season of unexpected amours. Mine silent, Bakhshi's overwrought, over-spoken, over-written. Mine that only a few people here noticed and that Chapla's friends in Kashi still seem to know nothing of; Bakhshi's that was the talk of the town and that everyone, far and near, has now read about in Jur'at Miyan's long poem.

Hazrat Khwaja Hasan was one of those itinerant poets who periodically descend in flocks on our city. Most of them come from Delhi, one step ahead of the troubles always raging there. Migratory birds, Sharad calls them, with the equanimity of someone who knows exactly where he belongs and doesn't intend ever to go far afield. When Delhi was laid waste Hazrat flew to Faizabad. There he teamed up with Miyan Jur'at, the blind poet who is senior to Mir Insha and Rangin, and a close friend of theirs. Miyan Jur'at and Hazrat moved to Etawah, then here, and they were soon to be seen wherever the beautiful people congregated. Our lane is of course one of those places. Two years earlier, Nadira had first told me about him: 'Hazrat Sahib invited Bakhshi to perform at his house last week and sent a couple of his students to escort her. A bunch of other girls went with her too. He and she had a long conversation. He seems quite smitten, one of the girls told me. Bakhshi has invited him over this evening. Come with me and watch the fun?'

I had been feeling a little cooped up so I agreed. We stepped into overpowering perfumes and a crowd of servants running around with flowers, fruit, wine, sweets. This was being treated as a special occasion, I realized. Bakhshi and two others performed to excellent effect, but I was watching him rather than her. The way he looked at her—I recognized that look. It meant that Dulhan was on the wane and Bakhshi was the new attraction of Mattan Apa's establishment. 'Better than the dancers at Indra Dev's court,' Hazrat exclaimed. 'A voice that carries one's life away,' added Miyan Jur'at. Dulhan busied herself making paan and tried to look unconcerned.

Hazrat was not young and was nothing much to look at, so his having lost his heart to the somewhat chilly and seemingly impervious Bakhshi was a bit of a joke for us girls. Especially because Mattan Apa, impressed by his elegant bearing, misunderstood the situation and thought he was a respected elder who would help her out by recommending

Bakhshi to the noblemen who mattered. She plied him with wine and delicacies, and requested him to treat the house as his own.

Hazrat took her at her word. He came every day and had long conversations with Bakhshi, much to Mattan Apa's gratification and our amusement. 'He weeps, he faints, he pines, see, see,' rhymed Shirin, unkindly. 'He must go, he must go to her alley,' Nadira rejoined. Bakhshi smiled, unmoved. 'He brings me lots of poetry books,' she said, as if in explanation. And he did indeed. She had a heap of them in her room. For the next two years, he kept coming and going, but Bakhshi seemed unchanged. She had tired of her first patron and left him, but was apparently in no hurry to find another.

But that summer, my summer, Nadira told me one afternoon, our usual time to chat, 'Bakhshi feels the same way Hazrat does.'

'Really? When did that happen?'

'Gradually, she says.'

I wrote to Chapla about it. 'The slow wick has finally caught. Perhaps it's true that if you focus all your attention on someone, they can't help noticing you.' Let it be true, said my heart.

'I wouldn't have thought Bakhshi had much passion in her,' I remarked to Nadira. 'She seems so placid, something like our Mahtab Baji.'

'Oh, she's much more gifted, there's no comparison, and when someone writes and sings as she does, there's an intensity smouldering within, you can be sure. Besides, she says they see the divine in each other.'

Things went on quietly for a while. Then one afternoon Mattan Apa came storming in. We heard her raised voice, joined by Mitthu's heightened cackling, and ran to Ammi's room. Sweat and the occasional tear trickled down Apa's face as she flopped against a bolster.

'Can you believe it? I thought he was going to introduce her to noblemen and instead the wretch was seducing her himself with his nonsensical talk of seeing divinity in her. The girl has gone mad. Look at my fate—this is Gulbadan all over again.' Was she glancing accusingly at me? Did she know that I had carried letters between Gulbadan and the English soldier she eloped with? 'She's the lamp of my old age; I wouldn't have cared if he'd taken to Nadira or even Dulhan. And I don't mind her spending time with him either, but not exclusively. Who does he think he is? He's just a poet, after all. Does he think I was born yesterday?'

'Took her long enough to find out,' Nadira whispered to me. My mind raced ahead—if they were ever to discuss Chapla and me, what would they say? Would I like them to discuss us? Yes, it would make us real. But, no, they would just laugh; there would be no drama. In any case, there was no 'us', just my many-coloured imaginings. 'What are you going to do?' Ammi asked consolingly, offering her the tray of paan, and signing to Heera to fan her.

'Oh, I've taken care of it, don't you worry.' She selected a paan with care, crammed it into her cheek, and wiped her face with the end of Ammi's light-as-air muslin veil. Her own was heavily embroidered with spangles. Ammi winced but Apa was oblivious. 'I sat him down today and told him he need not bother to show his face again. *Ishq* indeed!

There's no shortage of *ashiq*s at my place. He can take his poetry and his passions elsewhere. And the same goes for your friend Miyan Jur'at.' My mother looked taken aback at this abrupt redefinition of the poet as her friend alone. 'Plucking at his sitar as innocent as can be. He may be blind but I have both eyes open.'

'Blind, blind,' shrieked Mitthu.

'How did you find out?'

Apa looked around at us, sitting and standing in different parts of the room, and pursed her lips. 'Someone told me what was going on, thank God. The girl had stopped talking to other gentlemen who come by. All these silly friends of hers'—she gestured towards us—'were conspiring to keep it a secret. What do they care if our earnings dwindle to nothing? They don't have to feed and clothe everyone, I do.'

Nadira looked as if she would like to argue but had thought better of it. We slipped out to the gallery.

'Now what will happen?' asked Azizan, resting her sharp little chin on Nadira's shoulder. I found Azizan's habit of talking in questions almost as exasperating as her frequent interruptions when Nadira and I were talking, so I ignored her.

We found out more that evening, when Hazrat unexpectedly appeared at our door, and led Miyan Jur'at up the stairs. I had to look twice; Hazrat seemed half his size, pale, and the skin taut over his cheekbones. Ammi greeted them calmly and began to talk of Miyan Jur'at's new poems, but Hazrat's mind was otherwise occupied. He was constantly stepping out, on the pretext of going to the bathroom, and gazing from the gallery towards Mattan Apa's rooftop. Miyan Jur'at launched into a long philosophical speech about the mysteries of ishq, and how no one could quench its flame once the two met who were destined to meet. Into these sublime reflections he dropped observations less than sublime.

'She has a voice like Tansen and she dances like Saraswati,' he declared. 'A woman's beauty and a man's courage. Breasts like oranges and eyes like fish-pools.'

Ammi made polite sounds of agreement but the rest of us turned away to hide our smiles. These amusing juxtapositions, which he would later put into his poem, reminded us of the rumours about how Miyan Jur'at had lost his sight after he pretended to be blind in order to spy on the women in his friends' households. It was hard to take his flights of rhetoric seriously; his funny poems were more convincing. My thoughts strayed otherwhere. How hard it is to describe someone properly, even someone whose face follows you waking and sleeping. Like Miyan Jur'at, I too could only call up the clichés of poetry. Face like an oval moon. Hair like rain clouds. Eyes like light filtered through shaken leaves. Mouth like a half-blown rose. Neck like a goblet. The stature of a cypress. A mind like . . . too hard to find a comparison. My own mind continued to hum, seizing words and discarding them. Skin like creamy marble. Hands like blooming lotuses. Breasts like moons unseen . . .

What felt entirely fresh turned stale when I tried to put it in words.

Nadira nudged me.

Miyan Rangin's sidekick Ma'aruf had just come in. We all knew he had set his sights on little Azizan. Sure enough, when Azizan entered, Ma'aruf looked at her meaningfully; she blushed and went out as if to check on something. Here was potential for the entire drama to be re-enacted. Ammi signed to me with her eyes when Ma'aruf stood up to follow Azizan, so I had to go after them, though I was waiting for a chance to slip away to my room and re-read Chapla's latest letter for the fourth time.

Nadira came in next morning and I hurriedly slid the letter into a book. 'Look.' She held out a ghazal. 'Hazrat has asked Azizan and me to sing it.'

'So?' I wanted to get rid of her as quickly as possible. My letter was more interesting than yet another ghazal by Hazrat. 'Don't you like it?'

She sat down on my bed, in her usual corner, kicked off her slippers, pulled her feet up under her. This everyday occurrence, and for some reason even the shape of her toes and the way her slippers flew in different directions, irritated me out of all proportion but I didn't let it show. 'It's all right, but that's not the point. It's meant to send a message to Bakhshi.'

I saw where this was heading, and laid the book aside, resigned to listening and advising. 'You'd better be careful. Apa will be furious if she finds out. She already blames all of us, you know.'

'She's being unreasonable. It's not as if he's a pauper. And you have no idea how my Bakhshi is suffering. She just lies there quietly, not speaking. Miyan Jur'at says Hazrat cries all night. Tears must be a relief.'

'Yes, but Apa has bigger plans for Bakhshi.'

Nadira tucked the ghazal into her bodice. Her sweat would dampen and darken it, I thought crossly; that was why I hesitated to carry any of Chapla's letters in my bodice. 'Bakhshi is making her own plans,' she said. 'Look, here's a ghazal she wrote, for Shirin to sing here, so that Hazrat can hear it.'

'You've become quite the ghazal bearer. You know that ghazals composed in one kotha are not supposed to be sung in another. Ammi will never allow it.'

'No one needs to know, especially not Shirin, so don't tell her. I'm changing the poet's name in the last line to yours but Hazrat will still recognize it. I came here to tell you to keep quiet about all this, and let the ghazal be sung as yours.'

Before I could protest she got up and left. I forgot any misgivings in the pleasure of lying back with my letter.

Chapla was in Kalkatta and had met Plowden Memsahib there.

'Ganga-ji is here but looks different, darker, older. Which is strange because Kashi is so much older than Kalkatta, but the river, the sea, are older than both, I suppose. I saw the sea for the first time, with so many ships, different shapes, sizes, colours. I had no idea there were so many kinds of ships. How must it feel to sail away and look at the sea all around? Shut in, yet free. I picked up shells on the shore—pink, orange, green. I'll bring you some. Thousands of white shells must have gone into the plaster to make your city glitter the way it does—so new.'

New? By its present name perhaps, and certainly in comparison to Kashi, but there had been dwellers here for centuries, and I'd lived here most of my life, so I hadn't thought of it as new.

'Plowden Mem—she told me to call her Lizbeth though her name is Sufia— is very interested in our music. She tries to play our songs on her piano and wants to learn the words. She and her friends once dressed up as a group of dancers and singers and performed for their friends, she told me.'

This I remembered having heard before. A group of *firangi*s had dressed up that way here, the year they met Nadira's mother, Khanam Jaan, whom they called Taanee. The Plowdens admired her so much that when she died they buried her in their garden, so I suppose the imitation was meant to be flattering.

'They must have looked odd in our clothes. She certainly sounds odd when she tries to sing our songs. I don't think I'd like to wear English clothes; they seem uncomfortable. She's coming your way, I hear. Shall I come your way again or is it too soon?' I rolled over on my stomach and buried my head in a cushion.

Early next evening, Hazrat turned up. Heera, who had just returned from the market, put her arm through mine to detain me in the gallery and whispered in my ear. 'I saw him at the Jagtey Jot *dargah* this morning; you know Bakhshi Apa is always going there.'

'Bakhshi says just the sight of each other is enough for them,' Nadira explained to me next day, while we were feeding the pigeons on the roof and keeping an eye out for the alley cat. 'So they see each other at the dargah every second or third day. Hey, stop that,' she yelled down at the children who were chasing the hens round the backyard. 'It puts them off their laying.'

'He's a real Majnun,' giggled Shirin, her head popping up at the top of the stairs. 'He hardly eats, he won't drink any wine, and Miyan Jur'at says he hardly sleeps. The other day he fainted and everyone thought he was dying. One pressed his feet, another his hands, one put water in his mouth, another warmed his soles, someone held his head, and all cried, "Oh, Oh, what's happened?" Then, he suddenly sat up and said he would rather burn his house down and die in it than live without her. Can you imagine? At his age!'

Nadira giggled and I smiled too but felt a sinking in my stomach. To live without, for years and years—how would that be?

'What rubbish,' Ammi called, overhearing us from below. 'Miyan Jur'at is cooking up a succulent romance and adding spices and chillies. It's only in poems that people carry on like that for years. In life, they soon tire of it. Come down and practise your singing, girls. Stop chattering about other people's affairs.'

'And as for Bakhshi, don't tell Nadira but I think she's a secret drinker,' Shirin whispered to me, as we went down. 'He won't drink at all and she drinks too much. She seems quite out of her mind.'

A few days later we noticed that Mattan Apa had stopped dropping in for her mid-afternoon chats.

'Well, naturally, she doesn't like Ammi entertaining Hazrat when he's creating such chaos at her place,' Shirin remarked.

'Miyan Jur'at is a very old friend and any friend of his is welcome,' replied Ammi calmly. 'Mattan is an old friend too, but I can't close my doors to either of them just to please the other. She'll get over it. Paramours come and go; one can't stake friendships on their doings.'

'Well, at least Mattan Apa is still allowing Nadira to come to our place,' Shirin remarked.

'Mattan would never be so rude as to stop anyone visiting us, don't you know that?' Ammi retorted.

But did Apa know that Bakhshi's ghazals were reaching Hazrat and his reaching her, neatly folded up and tucked away in Nadira's bodice, and sung here by Shirin? She would certainly have objected to that.

In all this excitement, no one spared much thought for what Nafis was up to with the girl from Kashi. This suited me very well; the letters in my bodice went unnoticed even by Nadira. I had found a way to protect them by wrapping them in layers of the finest muslin, constructed from one of Ammi's old *dupatta*s. Against my skin I almost felt the paper she had touched, caressing me as I moved.

Were it not for the poem Miyan Jur'at later wrote about Hazrat and Bakhshi, I wouldn't remember the details of their story because from that first summer the only stories I stored up were the ones she recounted in her letters. The letters I wrote to her I can't remember, even though I spent so much time writing and re-writing each one, trying to sound eager but not too eager.

~

A month later, she wrote to say that she and her mother were coming to stay for a while. Ketaki Bai wanted a change of scene after her brother's death, and she wanted Chapla to pick up new techniques and perform here for the Nawab and his courtiers, and for the Resident Sahib as well. Years later, I found out that she also wanted to consult the English doctor at the Residency if she could manage it. I would have liked to think the visit was Chapla's idea but Chapla sounded distressed. 'I don't like being trundled about from city to city, leaving half my things behind while carriers damage the other half on their rickety carts. I want to settle down in one place. The good thing is, though, that I'll see you and we can continue the conversation we began. I remember your room full of delights—books, and sweets, and poems.'

I glanced round my room which had seemed far from delightful until a moment ago; now, it glowed. They were going to rent a couple of rooms in the small kotha that was squeezed between ours and Mattan Apa's, and that was rapidly declining in the face of the competition we presented.

Next door. She would be next door. We'd be practically in the same house. We'd be able to talk, gallery to gallery, or run up and meet on the rooftops. Was this what my life of half-fulfilments had been eddying towards?

They were supposed to arrive in the morning but it was raining, unseasonable early rains, and the alleys, narrow, criss-crossed, climbing, descending, full of potholes and brickbats, were flooded even by this brief shower. Rain is auspicious, but it would delay them. As I went through the motions of the day, I kept going to the nearest window at every unfamiliar sound. Nadira carried on with her routine, unperturbed. I wandered through the rooms prepared for them, fidgeting with various items, adding finishing touches, refreshing the water in the flower bowls, seeing her hands touch these familiar pieces of furniture borrowed from our house, her long, slightly splayed feet on these old rugs. Nadira kept a quizzical eye on me but said nothing.

It was evening when a hubbub announced they were here. I ran down behind a crowd of girls; the men were there before us, helping them alight. She flashed me a smile, while Ammi embraced her and the stately Ketaki Mausi, steel to Chapla's quicksilver. Wading through the swirling, muddy water, we ascended the narrow stairway next-door, while the carriers squabbled about the best way of getting their boxes up. Little Kishen was with them, a shy, still round-faced toy for the younger girls, who carried him off with squeals.

Weaving through the crowd, her glance, evanescent as a breath. Her eyes directly on me, just for a moment.

That night, a few yards of air, a few thin walls between us. After the mehfils were over, and everyone had gone to their rooms, I walked to the end of our gallery, leant over the parapet.

The waters had receded. Drifting from the front lane the sounds of men's quarrels; murmurs and snatches of song from rooms around me. Cats squabbling in the back alley. Miyan Ma'aruf reciting a bad *sh'er* in woebegone tones, followed by Azizan's laughter. The house vibrated with the unrest of young lives, like the string of a sitar gently plucked.

She was out of sight so the next best thing was to gaze at the house she was in. She was actually here but hadn't she always been somewhere very near, just out of sight? Occasionally, I heard Ketaki Mausi's voice and once Kishen's, complaining, but not hers. She must be asleep, having travelled for days, I thought. It grew later and later. The jasmine had recovered from the untimely rain, and flung its scent into the moist darkness; I could smell it all the way from Mattan Apa's. Even Dadda and the other nurses and maids, who stayed up later than the rest of us, chatting near the well in summer or round the fire in winter, had long gone to sleep.

I felt a bit like Mitthu. Pent up, jealous of the pigeons who could fly from roof to window to skylight, could peer into rooms at any hour and see what everyone was doing. Or if I were a moth, like those blundering at my window, trying to get to the candle within, I could reach her more easily. I wanted her eyes on me. Burning me free.

I expected a sign, but there was none. Finally, I scribbled a note, climbed up to our rooftop and down from theirs to her gallery, and listened at her door. Did I dare lift the latch? No, I didn't. I stood there for a long time, then slid the note under the door and left. Threw myself on the bed, having walked through a desert and not reached the oasis.

All of next day they slept, Heera reported. In the evening, at the mehfil, I sat, as usual, behind my mother and Shirin, who began singing together at someone's request. I was often an accompanying singer, but I felt shaky and excused myself, saying I had a sore throat. Chand was only too glad to take my place. The room was crowded; perhaps some hoped to see the newcomers, although Azizan was also profiting these days from Bakhshi's refusal to perform. I spotted Mir Insha, debonair in his rose-coloured *kurta* and saw something change in his eyes, change in the whole room. Everyone seemed to be looking at me, no, at someone behind me. I half turned, and an indescribable scent touched me—as if composed of light and water, the Gomti at dawn. A sari the pale gold of *ketaki* flowers, jasmine woven into the long plait that seemed to twine around her. Her eyes pleaded, hesitant, almost afraid. She leant forward a little, lips parted in a half-smile. For the first time, I understood the Braj poets comparing a girl to a creeper. Sinuous, but tougher than it looks.

Afterwards, when my mother's intimates congregated in her room to meet Ketaki Bai, Mir Insha patted my head. 'Has the little girl written any more poems?'

'No, but I will,' I said with uncharacteristic boldness, setting off a general laugh.

Mir Insha was one of my mother's friends. Old as he was in my eyes then, he yet looked like those cherubs that adorn the Nawab's ceiling—the naughty but somehow innocent smile, black eyes twinkling with mischief, dense curls that were beginning to recede, cheeks that seemed to invite pinching. Men, women and those in-between, all were charmed by him. It took years for me to realize that beyond the daggers of his repartee was the unexpectedly shy, sceptical patrician, easily bored, wary, but then with certain people, at certain times, opening up, brilliant as the sky.

Chapla took my hand and drew me out in to the gallery. How many times in the months after, she would do that, take my hand or arm and pull me gently, like a child leading a bemused adult. I would have followed her anywhere, blindfolded.

'Show me your books?'

I led the way, sure I would stumble at every step. She took a deep breath. 'Such a relief to be out of the crowd.' She moved restlessly round the room, opening and closing books, laying them aside, looking out of the window. 'Mir Insha's very clever, isn't he?'

'Very. And very good-hearted. But he gets taken advantage of, and misunderstood.'

'People must envy him. They must envy you too.'

'Me?' I couldn't help laughing. 'You're confusing me with my sister.'

'No, I'm not.' She changed the subject with an abruptness I would grow used to. 'If you didn't live here, where would you want to live?'

'Wherever you live,' I wanted to reply.

But I said, 'I don't know. Shahjahanabad, perhaps? And you?'

'In Vaishali maybe.'

'So long ago?'

'Yes, I should have liked to see Buddha. Or . . .' She hesitated. 'Maybe London a hundred years from now.'

'You want to be a *memsahiba* and talk *git-pit*?'

'Why not, for a change? Only it's too cold there. I wouldn't like that.' Then, with another shift, cajolingly, 'Show me some more of your poems.'

I gave her a couple of carefully selected sheets, and she sank to the carpet to study them.

'Will you help me improve mine?'

'*Islah*?' If I corrected her poems, would I become her teacher? The idea was seductive but also emphasized the age difference between us, and I didn't think I was a good enough poet to be a teacher.

'If I can. I'm not sure I can. And you'll read mine?'

'Of course.'

We had tied a knot of sorts.

'Have some *kheer*? Or some mango *kulfi*?' I touched her head lightly, as if touching a flame. 'Ammi made it for Mir Insha, it's his favourite.'

'All right.' She smiled up at me, teeth like pearls, no, teeth like the sun, blinding. For one so slim and fragile-looking, she had a hearty appetite, I would soon learn.

I turned, she caught my hand. This suited me, as I was sure I would trip, my head felt so light. 'Don't go. We can wait till someone comes.'

'Chapla, O Chapla!'

'Amma!' She pulled a mock-rueful face and stood up.

'You look very nice in a sari,' I said foolishly, feeling as if I was telling the moon he looked nice.

'I wore it for you,' she said, and disappeared.

I sat down, and tried to steady my brain by making lines rhyme.

I heard Mir Insha leave my mother's room, reciting a silly couplet about Ketaki perfuming Gul. He was always one for complex scents and intriguing odours.

She shushed him with mock-annoyance; her name is Gul-rukh.

3

Sharad came over early next evening, followed by Nadira, who wanted to borrow my mirror-work bangles. I was usually delighted when my little group gathered in my room, but today I was preoccupied.

'What's going on, Nafis Bai? You look as if you've seen a ghost,' Sharu remarked, running a hand through his long curls.

'Aren't you a little old for these ringlets?' I parried.

'You look like you haven't slept since last evening.' He was half-amused, half-curious, and he could always read my face. 'Did Ketaki Bai's daughter run away with your heart or what?'

I went out to the gallery and called Shirin to take her string of pearls that I had rethreaded. She appeared, half-smiling, half-pouting. 'You could have sent it through Heera—I'm aching all over, I need a massage. Those pesky kids let the hens out into the lane and I was the only one there so I had to catch them. Ammi's been looking for you, and you were here all the time. She's asking . . .'

'Ammi thinks I'm wasting her daughter's time, doesn't she?' Sharu asked, and began to sing a snatch of song about time passing and buds withering on the branch. 'But what are you up to, Shirin Bibi? Has the moon-faced prince been entangled or not?'

'He was entangled long ago,' Nadira replied archly.

'I mean entangled into moving her to the palace and having some sort of wedding.'

'Perhaps he's more like his uncle—gazing on whiter moons,' said Nadira.

Shirin pulled a face and clicked her tongue in annoyance.

'You mean John Mordaunt Sahib?' Sharu responded.

'Who else?'

'He has shapely legs,' Sharu conceded, still studying me quizzically. 'But he has an exhausting way about him. Always running around with guns or racquets and creating a ruckus.' We smiled. Impossible to imagine Sharu running around with anything, however gracefully.

'Some people find that exciting.'

'Mmh, white skins, most unattractive.' Sharu pulled a face. 'Anyway, he's of an age for the father, not the son.' Shirin looked gratified.

'I hear another moon-faced one has arisen in the firmament?' said Nadira.

'Yes, we told him to come tonight to hear Shirin Bai,' said Sharu. 'But I don't think he will; he's too much in demand. Of course, he's heard Gul Bai at court.'

'Who's he?' I couldn't help asking, though I was trying to divert attention from myself.

'He's called Ratan,' said Nadira, settling into the bolsters and the new topic, I saw with relief, as she began to make paan for Sharad. 'New boy from Ilahabad. Bakhshi saw him at the palace. She said he cast a spell over everyone, from the Nawab and the ladies to the hijras and jugglers.'

'Really? I hadn't heard that.' Shirin was not happy to be forestalled at palace news. 'And Bakhshi is back in circulation? So much for her highness's fits.'

'She was hoping Hazrat would be there,' said Nadira shortly. She had no patience with Shirin's jibes at her friend.

'Well, at least she seems to have got back her voice. You should have heard her the other morning.' Shirin lowered her voice to a groan and rolled her eyes up to the ceiling. '"Oh somebody, please help Bakhshi to meet Hazrat." As good as a play.' Nadira looked on the verge of losing her temper and I hastily intervened.

'What else did she say about Ratan?'

'He dances like an angel and not only that, he made everyone laugh, even Mir Mushafi who's generally so sour when Mir Insha is around. Must be quite something.'

'He is,' agreed Sharu, one of the few times I heard him praise anyone wholeheartedly. 'Very clever, and funny too. But not a show-off.'

'What's he like to look at?' asked Nadira.

'Quite spicy.'

'As beautiful as you?'

'That would be difficult!'

'Fair or dark?'

'Mm, golden, like wheat.'

I'm usually bored by discussions of shades of complexion that everyone finds so engrossing, but this time I was glad to have the topic introduced; it should be good for a few minutes' talk.

'Smooth as butter,' Sharad added. 'No one could take their eyes off him as long as he was there.'

I wished I could deflect questions by joking about my tastes, as Sharu was so good at doing, but I lacked the art.

'Even you?' Nadira was laughing.

'Naughty girl.' Sharu had picked up my mirror-ring and, since it was too small for his thumb, was holding it out at an angle to squint at himself and carefully disarrange his curls.

'Have you fallen for him?'

'No, my dear, I fell for myself long ago.'

They made for the door in a wave of laughter, and were intercepted there by Mir Rangin, who immediately plunged into recounting the foolishness of his one-time pupil Miyan Ma'aruf. The poets' conversations were sure, sooner or later, generally sooner, to veer around to their pupils, rivals, and pupils who had metamorphosed into rivals. Something about people in groups breeds the pleasures of backbiting—courtiers, poets, musicians, and all of us, we were all the same.

'He told me he's going on *umrah* next year,' Sharu interjected.

'Oh, so the cat goes on hajj after eating a hundred mice,' retorted Mir Rangin.

'He could hardly have eaten that many, poor fellow,' laughed Nadira.

'You're right, Nadira Bai, the mice turned into cats at the sight of him.' And Mir Rangin broke into verse, gesticulating as he recited.

Dilli mein Salamat thi tawaif mashhoor
Ma'aruf tha us par jaan aur dil se choor
Yeh to marta tha us par lekin Rangin
Voh kahti thi usko chal be chal door ho door

In Delhi lived a famous *tawaif* called Salamat
Ma'aruf was sold on her, life, heart and all
He was dying for her, but, says Rangin,
She said, Get lost, go on, away with you.

Through our laughter, in which Mitthu in the gallery joined with enthusiasm, we asked if this was a true story, and he assured us it was. 'Still, I shouldn't stay angry with him even though he spread lies about me and insulted me,' he added. 'He was my pupil, and a pupil is like a son. Once a son, always a son.' No doubt, I thought, the reason why so many sons don't speak to their fathers.

So Ma'aruf's new-found fondness for Azizan was not single-minded. No surprise there.

'But,' Miyan Rangin added, 'He doesn't understand how important my writing is. Before I die, I'm going to write the largest number of verses in the largest number of forms, more than any other living poet or even any dead one. I'm inventing all kinds of new forms, and I write in more than twelve languages.'

Here was something to discuss with Chapla—what did she think about quantity and quality in the writing of verse? How should I put it so that my wit would call up a smile? As a question or a comment?

Hazrat hailed them from my mother's room, and they surged out.

'Coming?' Sharad asked, still smiling wickedly. 'Or waiting?'

'In a few minutes. You go ahead.' He made a mock bow and left but I lingered though I could hear my mother singing. Would Chapla send a message or make some sign?

Instead, Nadira reappeared, fuming.

'Do you know who first told Mattan Apa about Bakhshi and Hazrat? It was your precious little sister. Heera overheard.'

'I wouldn't believe everything Heera says.'

'I believe this. Because I know Shirin.'

'But why would she do that?'

'Jealousy, what else? Shirin knows she doesn't have half Bakhshi's talent.'

The curtains parted and Shirin stormed in. 'I couldn't help hearing you, Naddo bibi, and it was bound to come out sooner or later. Apa's not blind. Even if she were, she'd have noticed the way Bakhshi was carrying on. And as for my envying her, didn't you see her rolling on the floor two days ago, laughing and crying and putting dust on her head? I'd be a fool to envy a crazy creature like her.'

Nadira looked startled; she hadn't expected to be overheard. 'We explained it as a jinn having possessed her,' she replied, stiffly.

'Right, Mahtab Baji already suggested that when all this started. So Apa went and brought an amulet from the Baba who sits at the Faizabad crossroad, but it only seemed to make her worse. She said she was burning up in the heat, she tore her shirt down the front, and tried to run out of the house. Someone had to tell Apa the truth.'

Nadira sniffed and said nothing. Satisfied that she had won this round, Shirin left.

I drew a deep breath. 'It really is hot; maybe that's why everyone is acting strangely,' I said. 'Did you notice how Mir Rangin was laughing at Ma'aruf for chasing Salamat when he himself chased Mahtab Baji in just the same way?'

'Yes, but that was long ago. One forgets.'

'How can you forget the way that you yourself felt?'

Nadira smiled and made herself comfortable on the divan. She's always prided herself on her maturity, although she's just my age. 'Everything fades with time, even feelings. Also, Mahtab Baji led him on, you know. She used to meet him openly as well as secretly every time she visited Delhi.'

Azizan had slipped in and was listening. We could hear Shirin singing now. Could one exchange two words with anyone without somebody, especially Azizan, listening in, I thought darkly. Trust her to show up wherever Nadira was. Her face was losing some of its baby roundness, and her figure acquiring curves, though she was still much too thin. 'Then what happened, Baji?' she asked.

'One day, he decided he couldn't bear the separation so he took the emperor's permission and rode all the way here to see her. Carrying perfumes and fabrics and ornamented slippers from Chawri Bazar that he couldn't really afford. He meant to surprise her but of course word reached her; rumour flies faster than horses. Mahtab Baji was careful to be out the day he got here. She told Khala Jaan to send him away.'

'But why did she do that if she used to meet him earlier?'

'She thought they were just having fun; she didn't realize that he would follow her here, expecting to set up a regular arrangement. He may write in twelve languages but he's a penniless poet. Let it be a lesson to you, Azzo—don't lead Miyan Ma'aruf on.'

'Not all poets are penniless. Look at Mir Insha. Doesn't he have elephants swaying at his door?'

'Now you're comparing a donkey with an Arabian.'

Azizan laughed uneasily and twisted her fingers together. On one shone an emerald that Miyan Ma'aruf had somehow procured for her. Probably pilfered from some elderly aunt of his. 'What happened next?'

'The door was bolted from inside, so he called out from the lane below. Khala Jaan looked out from a window, told him Mahtab Baji was out, and drew the curtain. He burst into tears and wrote a ghazal on the wall outside with charcoal. The kids crowded round and read it aloud as he was writing it, and they had a good laugh at every line.'

'A whole ghazal?'

'Yes. I remember only one couplet, though:

Ab hu'i ham ko sakht hairani
Chaah chitvan se us ne pahchani

Now I am deeply embarrassed
She saw desire in my gaze.

'But how could she see his desire when she wasn't there?' asked Azizan, with the literal-mindedness of a child, and I looked away, wondering if my feelings were inscribed on my face. Yes, Nadira could probably read me as easily as she could one of Mir Rangin's less clever verses.

'He first saw her when he was sitting on our rooftop, right?' Azizan asked.

'Yes, he was in town for a few days, and was drinking wine with Motilal Bajaj and Khan Sahib on our upper terrace one evening.' Nadira turned to me. 'And then Mahtab Baji came out on your lower terrace to take in some clothes that she had hung out to dry. They told him her name and he said she indeed looked like the moon that was rising. He recited this verse right away:

Thi shola ya voh barq ki ji mera jal gaya
Aisi hi ki nigah ki bas dam nikal gaya

Was she a flame or a flash of lightning - my heart burnt up
She glanced in such a way that my life left me.

To this I couldn't help responding. 'Mahtab Baji lightning! She's so slow, more like a wick that refuses to light.'

Nadira gave me a knowing look. 'Hmm, there are different kinds of lightning and they strike people differently. Well, I'd better get back or Khala Jaan will be cross. How come you're still here? Shouldn't you be singing with Shirin?'

'I'm going, I'm going. Let her finish singing Bakhshi's ghazal. I don't want to get involved with that mess you all have created so I didn't prepare it. Run along, Azizan, Miyan Ma'aruf must be waiting for you.'

And then, just as I was blackening my teeth and reddening my lips, preparing to leave, she looked tentatively round the door. My eyes widened with pleasure but she thought it meant this was a bad time and shrank back a little.

'Oh, you're going to the mehfil—I'll come later.' Her eyes wide too, like an alarmed squirrel's, her mouth pursed, a rosebud about to burst open.

She's stopped pursing her lips now—she's all grown up.

'No, no, it doesn't matter at all.' And it didn't; everything and everyone was neatly erased from my mind when she appeared. I put down the comb. 'Come in. What have you been doing?'

'Nothing much. Don't you find the day drags, particularly in the afternoon? It seems to go on forever. I feel worn out before evening begins.' She stepped in but stood poised to take off, a wild deer ready to flee at the slightest sound.

'Most of us sleep in the afternoon because we stay up so late at night. Don't you?'

'I can't sleep.' She looked down, hesitated. 'It's hard sleeping alone or with my mother.'

Turning away to choose bangles, I made a sympathetic sound. 'Why don't you ask Champa to come here?' Though this was the last thing I wanted.

'She can't. Her mother won't let her.'

'You're so thin, skin and bones.' Interesting, this reversal that was happening without my planning it; I was used to older women lecturing me on the need to fill out. 'It's probably hunger that keeps you awake. Come on, eat some of this.' I held out a morsel of the *lauki ka halwa* that Dadda had stashed in my room.

'You sound like my mother,' she laughed, opening her mouth nevertheless like a baby bird. Glistening channel, red *datura* flower that almost drew in my fingers along with the green sweetmeat but didn't, alas.

With a sudden change of mood, she started picking up pieces of jewellery from my silver tray—earrings, nose-pin, head ornament, and playfully sticking them into my hair, laughing as she did so.

I squirmed delightedly. 'What are you doing, silly girl?'

'Dressing you up. See—this green goes with that pink!' She pulled me down on the carpet. 'Let's play *chaupar*.'

'Now? Isn't your mother expecting you? I'm sure mine's expecting me.'

'We can make a late entrance. That's the way to attract attention, you know. Where did you get this set? It's gorgeous.'

'It belonged to my Nani in Shahjahanabad. Look, the pieces are girls, and their hair is filigree with real pearls. When you turn them over like this, their long skirts flop over and another head appears. The emperor gave it to her. It's one of the few things she managed to bring with her when they fled eastward.' I held one out and she took it, but her fingers didn't touch mine.

'Tell me more.' She leaned forward, supporting her chin on one long slender hand. 'Did you know your Nani?'

I began to talk, my eyes still on her creamy fingertips toying with the yellowing ivory.

The year was spent telling and listening. I became unusually loquacious, telling stories I'd never told anyone, repeating others that acquired different colours when told to her.

Her stories revealed both the heroine of a romance and a little girl in need of protection. At times intrepid and worldly-wise, telling me about her mother's suitors and hers, assessing and dismissing each one with practised acuity. But also frightened, anxious, lonely.

'You're so lucky to have nice neighbours,' she said wistfully one rainy day when Nadira had brought over hot almond milk because I had a cold. 'When I was a child we had an awful older neighbour. Thank God, she's gone away to live with her patron now. She used to beat me and pinch Kishen—he was a baby then and he was left with me a lot. She said he would die if I told anyone.' Her face shrank. 'And Amma was always away in other cities, so I didn't want to worry her.'

I wanted to unroll time like a scroll and rewrite it, go back and protect the child she had been. Did thinking about her fears help me bury my own, I wonder now, but, no, at the time I saw her, only her, everything coloured by and through her, and I temporarily disappeared except as the one pulled towards, rushing towards her. It was only when she was away for long periods that I had time to be anxious, afraid.

The first time I saw her dance in public was at Mir Rangin's house. That mehfil occurred soon after the famous contretemps about the scraps of cloth.

Ammi's good taste in clothing was much admired in our neighbourhood and I was said to have inherited her designing abilities.

'Make me something special for the trip to Banaras next month,' Shirin pleaded. 'I want the prince to notice me.'

I agreed absent-mindedly. But the job was not as easy as it seemed because Shirin was fussiness incarnate. Though I was supposed to be in charge she constantly interfered. We spent hours with our cloth dealer, Motilal Bajaj, and she wavered between fabrics until I was ready to scream. Finally, she chose a sunset pink with a green border. But the moment he left, her doubts began.

'Does it really look good on me?' She draped it over herself before the mirror. 'I think it makes me look pale. Chapla, what do you think?'

'It's very pretty,' said Chapla gravely.

'But don't you think it makes me look washed-out?'

'No, you look just as you always do.'

I smiled to myself at this clever response; Shirin's complexion tends to a bland white and Chapla's to a warm cream.

'I don't know—perhaps the turquoise and gray was better. It was sort of dull, though. Or do you think the dark red was best?'

'Motilal-ji won't take this back now it's been cut,' Ammi pointed out.

'Nafis Baji could have it. She hasn't had anything new since Id. It'll look good on her, she's darker than me.'

'Is it what you'd have chosen for yourself?' Chapla asked me later, as she stretched out on my rug.

'I don't know,' I said crossly. 'Probably not.'

'You should have said so, then.'

'Oh, Shirin always gets her way. And I don't care much about clothes.' This wasn't quite true any more, since as I got dressed each day, I knew she might see me. 'Can I look at this on you for a minute? Shirin is about your height.' She stood up. 'Turn around.' My hands on her shoulders, tingling to follow the fabric as it undulated over her. I pulled back abruptly. 'That'll do.'

After I had designed the red outfit, pairing it with black and gold, and had spent a good deal of time hunting in various shops for the right drawstring and spangles, and then explaining the design to our Mughalani, another storm erupted. Shirin went to a mehfil at court and returned like a whirlwind, wailing at the top of her voice. We all rushed to her room, the girls followed by two dogs and a baby deer, Mitthu agitatedly flapping his wings in the gallery, no doubt wishing he could come too.

'Dulhan Apa was there, wearing exactly the same thing. With the same trimmings.'

'The same as what?'

'As my new outfit that you're getting stitched, what else?'

'How's that possible?' I said. 'I didn't buy the gold brocade. I cut it out of Ammi's old *peshwaz* from Delhi that's fraying. And it's been in Mughalani's sewing room since it left mine. There's no way she can have exactly the same thing.'

'All right, so it wasn't exactly the same. Don't be so literal, Baji. It was almost the same. The red was the same fabric, and so was the black. The gold was very similar. And they've done this kind of thing before.'

She turned to Mahtab Baji who was engaged in gently abstracting a saffron-hued *sandesh* from a pot that a Bengali admirer of Shirin's had brought her to celebrate the birth of his first son. Kishen eyed the sweet in her hand and then turned his attention to a glass of stale wine Shirin had left on a low table. Chapla, who always seemed to watch him from the corner of an eye, however absorbed she might be elsewhere, scooped him up.

'You remember your cream *kurti* of French gauze with the little pink roses, and how Bakhshi Apa turned up at a court mehfil last year in the same thing before you could wear it?'

Mahtab Baji nodded placidly. 'Yes, that was a bit odd but I thought it was coincidence. Anyway, she wore hers with silver and I wore mine with pink so they looked quite different. I didn't mind.'

'It wasn't coincidence. They're doing it deliberately. I tell you, they somehow manage to see our clothes while they're being stitched.'

'That's impossible,' I said.

'Oh, is it? How do you know Nadira Baji isn't telling them? She spends half her time with you, after all.'

'Don't be ridiculous. You think Nadira has nothing better to talk about than your outfits?' Shirin cast a suspicious glance at the little ones who were playing in the gallery with scraps collected from Mughalani's room, pretending to decorate a house; Kishen had wiggled away from Chapla and was tying strips of many-coloured cloth to the railings. I glared at her, daring her to mention Chapla who was also in and out of both houses.

She backed down but not entirely. 'Anyway, I can't wear it now.'

'Whyever not? It's for Banaras and Dulhan Apa's not going there.'

'I don't care whether she's going or not. It'll look as if I copied her outfit. Someone or other is sure to report it. Everyone will laugh at me.'

'I can change the trimming. Mughalani has some green satin left over from your Id set, and there's the pearl edging from . . .'

'No, I won't.' She burst into tears and threw herself on the bed. 'Ammi, I won't wear it, I won't. I won't go to Banaras at all if I have to wear it.'

'All right, all right, calm down, bitiya. Nafis, is yours done yet?'

'No, Mughalani hasn't had time. She's trying to finish Shirin's.'

'Then would you mind switching with her again?'

'I don't think Shirin's will fit me.'

Mughalani had come in by now, attracted by the uproar and was complaining about the pilferage of her work to Dadda, Heera, and whoever else would listen.

'It's only half done. I'll cut it short and fix it for you, bitiya, don't worry,' she assured me, as if I was the one insisting on the exchange. 'I always leave plenty of space in the seams.'

I agreed but I'd lost interest by this time, thinking of something quite different—what would Chapla say when she read my new poem about Ganga and Gomti meeting and embracing? She had described Kaithi to me, the place where they meet. 'We stopped there on our way to Prayag for the Magh Mela,' she had written to me. 'Such serene whiteness—flat sands stretching out to the groves and fields, white flowers growing wild, and flocks of white birds diving down to the laughing water. I liked the dolphins best—whole bunches of them with long beaks like birds, gambolling and leaping in the river. They have smiling faces. Amma picked up a sharp shell on the shore to cut vegetables with. We went to the temple of Markandeya Rishi, who is forever sixteen. His parents chose a short life and brilliance for him over a long but undistinguished life. Shiv-ji gave him immortality. Brilliance makes you immortal if you don't care about a long life.' My ghazal was about merging with another, becoming immortal by losing one's life, one's self. Would she mind my interweaving her words with mine? Would she like my fairly obvious allusion or would it displease her?

A few days later the mystery was solved when Nadira dropped in and announced, 'It's Sundari's doing.'

Sundari was the young cleaning woman. Several girls appeared, all agog.

'What's her doing?' I was bewildered.

'Where do you live, Nafisan? Come out of your poetry books once in a way, won't you? The business of the copied clothes, of course.'

'How could Sundari have copied them?'

'She didn't copy them. She's been saving the scraps of cloth she collects from your Mughalani's sewing room when she sweeps it and then taking them over to our seamstress to copy your choices and combinations.'

'*Ha'i Dayya*!' Overcome by this revelation, Mughalani sat down with a thud while the rest shook their heads at such perfidy.

'Oh, that treacherous little thing! Let her come, I'll scratch her eyes out, I'll beat her up with my slippers. How dare she?'

'Shirin, mind your language,' said Ammi. 'You're not a prostitute in the market fighting over a client.'

Kishen came in, tugging Chapla by the hand behind him.

He spread his arms wide. 'Saw a *hu-u-uge* carriage,' he said. Why are boys of all ages so taken with vehicles? Most of the girls started laughing and cooing at him, and lost interest in the fracas.

'Apa and Bakhshi say they admire your clothes because Khala Jaan and Nafis have such good taste, so they wanted to use them as models, that's all,' continued Nadira. 'They didn't mean to compete with you.'

'Right,' sniffed Shirin. 'They can go tell that to whichever fool will believe it. I wasn't born yesterday.' She didn't quite say that Nadira must have been in on the secret but she implied it.

'They probably paid Sundari,' agreed Heera.

'Not the right way to behave,' pronounced Ammi. 'How would they like it if we copied their songs?'

This quieted Shirin down, and we avoided each other's eyes.

'Anyway, now Nafis has something new to wear for the mehfil at Mir Rangin's house,' said Mahtab Baji, always ready to smooth things over. 'You'll be away, Shirin, so Nafis will have to take your place.'

The distraction worked. 'Will you come along with us and dance, Chapla beti?' asked Ammi. 'It's just a small get-together of his friends.' It wasn't quite clear which kotha Chapla was attached to, since she wasn't a permanent resident and was staying in the house between our two establishments. She looked across the room, read my face, and replied, 'Whatever you say, Khala.'

A chance to perform with her, in front of everyone!

She put her hand on Kishen's forehead and exclaimed. He had been out in the heat and had fever again, she said, so she carried him away. I probably wouldn't see her till the next day, I thought. But in the early evening, the curtain stirred. My heart jumped but I gave no sign. As I went through my papers, selecting songs, she came in quietly and sat down on the floor to redden her heels and colour her toenails. She was treating my room as her own, I realized, my heart beating faster. Had I ever seen such perfectly curved nails, each like a little mirror? No colour could improve their sheen.

'Why are you doing that? I can ask Heera or one of the younger girls to do it for you.'

'I like doing mindless tasks. Calms me down. Listen, if I'm going to dance could you sing Nazir Akbarabadi's "Pari ka Sarapa"? I know that one well. Oh, good evening, you . . .'

The children's pet deer was nuzzling her shoulder. Animals and children were drawn to her like metal to a magnet.

Everyone knew that head-to-toe eulogy of a young dancer, but I had something else in mind. It would be a surprise compliment to the host to sing one of his poems instead; it too was a *sarapa* of a girl but in a female voice, a woman singing to a woman, so it would serve a double purpose, especially as it compared the girl to the red fairy. I thought Chapla was skilled enough to dance impromptu to it, so I didn't rehearse it with her.

On the big day Ammi had a headache and decided not to come, so Mahtab Baji was in charge of our group. Mahtab Baji neither danced nor sang particularly well; just conversing in a languid fashion seemed to work for her. 'That red actually looks lovely on you,' Chapla said, popping in while I was getting ready. Her eyes running over me made me shy and I turned away. Did she remember that I was in red the first time she saw me?

'Here, let me try something different with your hair.' She came up behind me and began to rebraid it. Any number of girls had braided my hair and I theirs but never had I felt their touch burn through me and reach ears, lips, eyelids, fingertips.

'Why aren't you dressed? What are you going to wear?'

'An orange and gold I've worn only in Kashi. Doesn't take me long to dress.'

'Oh, can't you wear red?' I was disappointed. 'You painted your toenails red so I thought you'd wear that red Murshidabadi silk you asked Mughalani to alter the other day.'

'Two reds?' She was amused. 'Wouldn't that be a little too much? Anyway, orange is close enough to red.'

'All right then, at least wear these.' I scooped up my fish-shaped earrings and gold bead bracelets and poured them into her palm.

'But why? They're so pretty. Don't you want to wear them yourself?'

'No, you wear them. They're lucky. Also, the fish is our city's emblem, you know, and this is your first public performance here.' I had last worn them the day I first met her.

'All right. I'm somewhat nervous, to tell the truth. I'd better go and get ready.'

As we descended the stairs to get into the palanquins, she smiled at me through the small crowd of girls. She had blackened alternating teeth so that the white ones shone like stars on a moonless night. For the first time I understood why they call us fairies. I leant back for a moment, hiding my face, but the others seemed unaffected, chattering and squealing.

Mir Rangin was at his door, with a glittering scarf on his head, bowing to welcome us. We entered the large front room and fell silent because a number of men we didn't know were greeting us. Had Shirin been there she would have continued to giggle and make eyes but we sat quietly, looking down. Then Mir Insha came in and dissolved the silence in a moment.

'*Arey*, no Gul-rukh Bai? The garden is perfumeless without flowers. On the other hand, there are two moons, so I'm confused.' He bowed elaborately to Mahtab Baji and Chand. Mahtab Baji is known as Farkhanda outside our close circle so several people missed the pun on the two names as well as his next sally: 'And the poet and her inspiration are here as well,' smiling at Chapla and me. 'Come on, what are we waiting for?' He took the *sarangi* from Chand and ran his fingers over it. 'I know how to play many instruments. You should have heard me on the sitar in my youth!'

'Yes, yes, do play. We'll be honoured,' several others chimed in. While Mir Rangin was supervising the refreshments, Chand and I began to sing, and a few others danced.

For a while, Chapla sat still, then she stood up and glided over the floor. Everyone broke out in exclamations of delight. Almost surprising myself by my boldness, I slipped into Mir Rangin's ghazal. Startled, he looked up. Chand, surprised, fell silent, and Mir Insha, smiling mischievously, swayed and nodded. Chapla looked taken aback and her skin warmed slightly, the way water does when you pour wine into it, but she kept up with me.

Hai zanakhi meri voh lal pari
Ho jise dekh nidhaal pari

Voh charhi gaat, vaah ji takhti
Voh parizaad chhab jamaal pari . . .

Kheenchi kanghi sitam o dheela pench
Zulf naagin syaah baal pari

Donon abru dhu'an ajab gardan
Saari nakh-sikh durust chaal pari

Bolna khoob roothna achha
Hansna bedaad aur malaal pari

Daant khaase dhari tilism jami
Suthre lab tis pe bol chaal pari

Bolna khoob roothna achha
Hansna bedaad aur malaal pari

Chhalle tasveer machhliyaan barraaq
Chooriyaan sabz haath lal pari

Nauratan zor dhukdhuki aafat
Nath ghazab pahunchiyaan sudhaal pari

My *zanakhi* is the kind of red fairy,
The sight of whom makes languid any fairy.

That swelling bosom, magnificent breasts!
Fairy-born, with the beauty of a fairy!

A comb pulled back, loosely coiled tresses,
Locks like a female cobra—a black-haired fairy! . . .

Her eyebrows captivating, her neck unique,
All her features perfect, her gait a fairy's.

Fine teeth, blackened with magical lines
Elegant lips, words and ways of a fairy

She speaks well, and gets annoyed well,
Her laugh incomparable, her melancholy a fairy's . . .

Her rings a picture, fish-shaped earrings brilliant,
Her glass bangles green, hands a red fairy's

Nine-gem necklace and pendant gorgeous
Nose-ring breathtaking, gold bead bracelets a fairy's

She glanced at me, realizing what I'd done. I paused, catching my breath, hoping she wasn't annoyed. Her eyes smiled—amused? flattered?—and I continued. It was a longer song than I was used to singing alone, but I managed, and Mir Rangin looked gratified.

Naaz toofaan kashmah shahar aashob
Ghamzuda zulm aur ada kamaal pari

Kurti naadir karaake ki mahram
Qahar pajama sar ki shaal pari

Paon pakeezah kafsh maahi pusht
Qad o qaamat ajeeb chaal pari

Qundaq paa hain odiyaan rangin
Al gharaz hai voh bemisaal pari

Her airs, a miraculous tempest, destroy the city;
Her grief afflicts one, each movement a fairy's

Her shirt exquisite, bodice splendid,
Pajamas wreak havoc, the shawl on her head a fairy's

Her feet pure and lovely, high-heeled shoes fish-patterned,
Height, figure and unusual manners a fairy's

The tips of her toes are 'colourful', Rangin,
Truly she's an incomparable fairy.

A storm of applause broke out, directed at Chapla, Mir Rangin and me. She sank down beside me and whispered, 'You're much naughtier than you seem, aren't you?'

~

Happenings, dates, words, objects that once seemed seared into my brain have vanished. Writing brings some of it back, first a mild warmth, then reflected heat. But what I record obscures the simmering depths. How little I know of what there was between us or what lay buried in her, how little I knew even then.

Most of it is lost forever. How much lingers in others' memories? What does Dadda, for instance, recall of our outings—when we would sit close together in the palanquin, giggling, as she stolidly followed on foot? With infinite caution my arm would slide round Chapla's shoulders and slowly relax there. As we travelled to Sharad's village one day through light rain, flame-like *palasa* flowers shone on both sides of a road that was little more than mud and stones but seemed like the road to paradise. Later, when we walked in his orchard we picked them up from the grass, and she rested her arm on my shoulder, which she was just the right height to do. I collected some in my dupatta to give to our Munshi-ji whose mother used them to prepare medications.

'Just like Mitthu's crest,' I said, admiring the glaring colour against the green.

'That's why it's called the parrot tree,' she said. 'Pick some more. I want to dye a bodice that flame colour. And here, taste this.' She plucked one from a low-hanging branch, snapped off the stalk, and tipped my head back, cradling it in one hand. I opened my lips and she squeezed the stalk, dripping honeyed drops on to my tongue.

Does anyone remember our eyes meeting across crowded rooms, as wine and conversation flowed? Nadira? Sharu? Often, she would signal that she was tired of her admirers and wanted to slip away and sit somewhere, complain of them and recuperate before returning. And who better to slip away with than me, whose absence few would notice? Other times, even on the same evenings, she seemed to thoroughly enjoy flirting with those same admirers, each glance, each laugh a dagger sweetly piercing.

At the time I thought only I was aware of her constantly recurring melancholy, when she would try to hide and brood, so hard to do in our household, maybe in any household. She would retreat to my room where she could conceal herself briefly, but perhaps she had other retreats too.

'I get so tired of people,' she said once. 'There are so many of them. Too many little men. I wish I could go away somewhere and just see you when I want to, and Champa when I want to. And sometimes my family. Get up in the morning, read and write by myself, practise, go for a walk, maybe see someone in the evening, eat, and go to sleep. Perhaps life in an ashram would be good, but even there there'd be too many people. I'd like to have a cave in the mountains.'

For these fugitive feelings poetry became a vehicle—a way of revealing and concealing. We constantly exchanged poems, folded into books, slipped from hand to hand, left under pillows. There was a time when each line she wrote was inscribed in my eyes, throat, heart, although I managed to slide over what I wanted to avoid. When I re-read them now, some I remember, others not at all.

I commented on her poems, suggested changes. One had my name in it, and I suggested removing it. She did, and now I wish I had let it remain. But she'd probably have removed it later anyway.

I told her everything, the past, the present, and she told me, it seemed, everything too. Bearers of each other's secrets. Unsteadily balanced on a cliff, looking into a chasm. When a mine of jewels reveals itself, obscure recesses glinting—is there any thrill like it? Tahmasp passing through the underwater cave where the vision of Shahmaran bursts on him, enthralling, wise, serpentine. But within that cave other caves, other beings unseen, other stories untold.

Those were not the first such poems, the first such letters I wrote. The first were to the Ustani who tutored all of us. She was a widow and lived with her younger friend and one-time pupil Shakuntala a few streets away. Everyone in the neighbourhood knew the story—how Shakuntala's husband was always either away on business or drinking with his associates and expecting her to cook for them. One day, he returned to find the entire house stripped, from ceiling to floor. Our Ustani had proved a good teacher; the two of them had removed curtains, carpets, every scrap and fragment, pot and pan, even taken away his slippers. One summer when I was very young and they seemed old but were actually much younger than I am now, Shakuntala went to visit her parents in the village and I suddenly noticed our Ustani in a new way. I started dropping in on her every day. I'd hang around, look through her books though I could only read a couple of the languages, scrutinize her pictures as if they could tell me of her past, leave poems under her pillow, and occasionally stay the night. She was flattered enough to respond a little, but mostly with cryptic remarks like, 'Rain has to fall at the right season. However much it may rain out of season, no crop will grow.' They have both moved to Shakuntala's village home now that her parents are gone.

The next summer, I wrote yet more poems, to Mattan Apa's niece Gulbadan who was visiting her. Small and round, flower-faced, flower-bodied, a chin flawless as fresh cream when she looked upwards. Her name being so close to my mother's was strangely tantalising. I would hang about outside her door in the dark, waiting to steal a kiss, and for months after, carried messages between her and an English soldier, while writing poems about my torment. Finally, she ran away with him, the year after Nadira's mother died. But why do these seem like old spelling books now, which I have no interest in re-reading? Perhaps because you may sing for many people, but the one you remember is she whose voice joins yours.

Everything else must have gone on as usual, but I don't remember the details—the mehfils, Rangin Sahib, Mir Insha, Madan, Sharu coming and going, along with noblemen and traders and soldiers of fortune, while I managed the accounts and the stores, kept an eye on the girls' connivances and the servants' conflicts. Like lanterns bobbing on bullock carts as they run through the dark, all I remember are moments—meetings, partings, writing verses and poring over hers late into the night.

Ammi was wholly occupied with Shirin who wanted her patron, the Nawab's nephew Ghaziuddin, exiled in Banaras, to marry her. Did Shirin sense the unlikely course by which he would end up coming to the throne? At that time, he was just the rather dull son of the Nawab's estranged brother. But when the Nawab died, the English decided that his volatile adopted son, Wazir Ali, didn't count, so they disinherited him and recalled Ghaziuddin's father to take over. Wazir Ali was enraged and killed Cherry Sahib who had delivered the order to depose him. Thousands rallied round Wazir Ali but he was defeated. Because of all these unexpected events, Ghaziuddin, some years later, became Nawab after his father.

Nadira paid less attention than usual to my goings-on because in addition to Bakhshi's affairs, she was busy with a courtier from Hyderabad who was wooing her. He came every evening to visit and brought expensive gifts, apart from keeping their kitchen stocked. She still has the heavy pearl bracelet although she rarely wears it; most of the other things were sold to tide them over various crises. Nadira was in two minds about him; he had a stutter and a stare that got on her nerves. On the other hand, she wasn't growing any younger, as Mattan Apa kept reminding her, and he had only one wife and a position at the Nizam's court.

Even so, everyone knew Chapla was in my room almost every day. Ammi and Shirin were both somewhat star-struck by her but the other girls had mixed feelings and let me know it. One day, we were on the roof, playing with the pigeons.

'She's a cold fish, don't you think?' Chand remarked as she tried to train a young speckled bird, tossing it up into the air and then calling it back as it ascended and circled.

'No, just reserved,' I retorted.

'Thinks too much,' Nadira said, caressing her mother-of-pearl hued Motiya. 'Like you.'

'Don't you feel she's acting a part, always hiding something?' put in Azizan, who was seated on a piece of sacking, feeding bits of grain to the birds on her head and shoulders.

'She has everything – beauty, breeding, intelligence,' Chand agreed, 'but still it's as if she's afraid to show her self.'

'Except maybe to Nafis.' That was Nadira again.

'She's shy,' I repeated. And afraid, I thought but didn't say, because I didn't quite know the answer to the question it would invite.

Nadira looked at me quizzically. 'Not as shy as you. And no one thinks you disguise yourself.'

'There are different kinds of shyness. She's going to be famous, that makes one shy.' That she both thirsted for and shrank from attention I didn't want to reveal; it felt too much like myself, my own secret.

'She's a pretty girl, and clever too,' said Mahtab Baji in her slow, caressing tones. 'She's always courteous; one can see she's been raised by a well-educated mother.'

'She has to return to Kashi one day,' Ammi, who was drying her hair in the morning sun, remarked with unusual mildness. 'What will you do then?' I didn't reply; after all, people did move from one place to another. Hadn't my mother? Hadn't Mir Insha, Rangin Saheb, Jur'at Miyan and Hazrat? Why should she return to Kashi at all?

That was also the year Ratan took the city by storm. Within a few months he seemed to know everyone and had set them all talking about him.

'A second Tabaan,' Mir Insha called him, smiling with the air of one who has seen better things. 'Except his poetry is in his body.'

'Mir Abdul Ha'i Tabaan, the poet? Didn't he die before you were born, Mir Sahib?' asked Ammi.

'Yes, but I knew those in Delhi who had seen him. I met the great faqir, Mir Mazhar Jaan-e Jaanaan, to whom Tabaan was very close, you know. I was young then and

Mazhar Sahib was old. I thought, why should I miss the chance to meet such a great man? So I went and visited him, and he told me a lot about Tabaan. He was living in a house that one of his followers, a Bania, had given him, deep in the alleys around Chandni Chowk. My elephant had trouble making its way there. I remember it as if it was yesterday, how he got up and greeted me, with that old-world civility. He was in white, with a samosa-shaped scarf, and I in a red scarf with a dagger shining at my waist. He was an admirer of beauty. No one could be his follower unless they first shaved their faces and became smooth like mirrors.'

'Mir Insha was a fairy-faced one,' Miyan Jur'at put in. Everyone except Chapla knew the story he was going to tell. 'When he was a young lad at the Emperor's court in Delhi, he recited this verse: *Gar nazneen ke kahne se maana bura ho kuchh/ meri taraf ko dekhiye main nazneen sahi* (If you're somewhat offended at my calling you a sweetheart/ Take a look at me, I don't mind being a real sweetheart). The great poet Sauda was there, and he smiled and said, "You are, you are, without a doubt."'

Mir Insha looked self-conscious, Chapla and I smiled at each other. Yes, he had everything required to be a fairy-faced one—fair, with refined features that were just starting to loosen as his hair receded. But his wit still dazzled. And his smile.

'Tabaan was much more beautiful than Ratan, wasn't he?' Ketaki Mausi asked.

'Who can measure or weigh beauty, Bai—which is more beautiful, the rose or the narcissus? But yes, he was so beautiful that even when he was grown-up and pursuing other beauties, he was still pursued. White as milk, and he always wore black, only black, so he looked like the moon in a midnight sky. Once, the Emperor himself sent word that he wanted to see him, so he sat outside his house and the Emperor rode by. Such beauty is not meant to grow old. It can only be snuffed out like a candle. Ratan is golden, a golden pearl.'

'Or a sunset cloud,' Sharad put in, almost to himself. My friend was certainly smitten.

'To cool down the over-heated,' teased Mir Insha, and Sharad joined the general laughter.

Surprising when I think of it now, I saw Ratan only twice, briefly. The first time was in a darkened room at the palace, after a session where Ammi and her cousin, Dilsukh Mama, had sung together to acclaim. Some of us were sitting and talking, with just one candle lighting the room, and Ratan knelt before me and talked for five minutes or less. Because I was Sharu's friend, I think. All I remember is a sense of white fizzing light in a dark space, and laughter spreading in circles round him. Like Chapla, he had the gift – or was it a curse? - of drawing everyone's eyes as soon as he stepped into a room.

My suitor, Madanmohan, served to fan Ammi's flickering hopes for me. She preferred him to visitors like Sharad, who she knew had eyes only for the boys. Madan's attentions were flattering, he was easy to talk to, and he was obliging if somewhat careful with money. I was still young enough to require an escort so I would sometimes go with him in search of special little things I wanted. That year, most of them were presents for Chapla, a silver pin for her hair, a *baadla* brocade bodice which I thought was a pretty allusion to her name, a notebook for her to write verses in. Procuring these things was easier than giving them, because a sort of paralysis overtook me when the moment came. I would resort to putting something in her hand just as her palanquin was about to move away or as we said goodnight at her door.

Madan found our friendship charming and observed us in a pleasantly mystified way. It was he who arranged our excursion to the new Imambara with its vast maze. But he didn't come himself; he was always on edge in groups, and preferred to meet me alone or just with her.

Sharad took to the idea at once and got everyone together. My efforts to manoeuvre her into my palanquin failed and I saw her wickedly laughing face flash by with Sharu smiling beside her. Like male and female versions of the same picture, albeit one much older than the other.

'The beautiful ones,' Nadira remarked placidly, snug beside me. 'At least, we don't have their worries.'

'What worries?'

'Oh, having to choose between scores of admirers.'

'How's Akbar Ali Sahib?' I asked quickly, turning away from her to peep out at the street.

'Very well. He wants me to go to Hyderabad with him.'

'Really?'

'Yes. He wants a *muta'a* marriage.'

'What do you think of that?'

'I prefer it to a *nikah*, because I need not renew a *muta'a* if I don't like living with him whereas with a nikah I'd be stuck until he released me. But I don't think I want to go so far away.'

'What does Apa think?'

'She thinks if he gives me a house so that I can live separately from his wife, it would be all right.'

At any other time, the idea of not seeing Nadira every day would have sent me into a panic. We had scarcely ever spent more than a week apart and had always told each other everything, or almost everything. As Sharu once inelegantly remarked, 'You think you can do without her but if she disappeared you would feel as if your room was stripped bare.' But right now it felt as if her going would free Chapla and me from constant observation. The simultaneous nearness and distance was becoming hard to take, like the scent of rose water during a fast.

That was the first time I saw the completed Imambara, on which the Nawab and his companions had spent hundreds of thousands—all, it was said, in order to give work and food to the drought-stricken poor. It had taken years to complete, the biggest, grandest building I'd ever seen. We were among the lucky ones during the drought. We were careful with water but we never lacked it. But thousands of poor peasants from miles around flocked to the city to work for food. We heard that some respectable gentlemen of our acquaintance disguised themselves to work at night on these buildings.

Coming from our comfortably crowded, narrow streets into these spaces and vistas, these impossibly high ceilings and gateways broad and solid as rock caverns, it felt as if here was the city's answer to the rivers, low hills and plains that surrounded it. Walking up scores of shallow steps to the great chandeliered hall was like ascending a hill. Except that the huge, half-smiling pairs of fish on the gateways above, sometimes curving towards, sometimes away from one another, had little to do with hills.

She looked up at the balconies towering round the stepwell. While others exclaimed at the marvellous ingenuity by which the guards far away in their east-side balcony could see anyone at the gate reflected in the water below, she seemed a little sad. 'I wonder if the *baoli* was here before they built this huge structure around it,' she said. 'This one has steps on four sides. Ours have steps on three sides.' What did it feel like to always see scenes elsewhere, I thought, I who had never been far from home.

The maze didn't remind her of anything, because none of us had seen anything like it, though Ratan had told Sharu about ancient ones in the Dakkan. A *bhulbhulayya* indeed, where any step can be forgotten, every turn lures one to escape the light, to venture just a little further into the narrowing shadows of dark passages, hoping that an unimaginable path lies round the corner, a tunnel leading to another road, another city, glimpsed through windows looking out on unfamiliar views, dead-ends where one may rest unobserved.

I'd had visions of her getting lost in the maze and running into my arms in some narrow channel, but instead we all stayed together and Nadira as usual ended up holding my arm until we stepped out on the enormous, rectangular rooftop. I unlinked myself as soon as I could and gravitated to the gallery that ran along the four sides of the rectangle.

Perfectly balanced, the arches, the domes, the fretwork repeated all around. In one of the open archways topped by a dome she stood, drenched in sunlight, silhouetted against the sky. I went up to her, a filing drawn by a magnet, and we gazed at the city, spread before us, and beyond, quiet fields and groves stretching to sky's end.

'There's a tunnel to Faizabad somewhere here, isn't there?' she asked, without turning.

'So they say, and others to Kalkatta and to Delhi.'

'We should find one and run away.' She turned, smiled impishly at me. Did she say these things just to make my heart speed up or did she partly mean them?

Maybe she wanted not so much to run away with me as to run away from others. So it seemed a few days later, when she and I strolled around a grassy thicket of boulders and small trees near the Gomti while Dadda fried pakoras on a wood fire, Kishen trotting up with twigs to keep it going.

'You know Panna Lal?'

I'd seen him but taken no notice of him—a thin, dark, pock-marked young trader who talked too much.

'He wants to set me up in one of his houses in Rampur.' She idly trailed a flower across my neck as she scanned the clouds. 'Looks like it might rain a little.'

'No, I don't think those are rain-clouds. But what about Mir Yusuf Khan?'

He was a distinguished nobleman from Pratapgarh whom I saw going next-door almost every evening these days.

'Hmm, yes, he wants me to marry him. He's an odd one. His wife died young and he never remarried.'

'Sounds ideal.'

'I don't think I want to get married, at least not now.'

'And he's so old.'

'That might be an advantage. Young men tire one out. Oh, let's not talk about this - it makes me sad; it's like talking to my mother. Tell me a story.'

'What sort of story?'

'A story about you. Tell me how you met Nadira.'

'I don't really remember meeting her. She's always been here, two doors down. I remember when we were quite small, the other girls would tease her for being dark. She'd sit there with big tears rolling down her cheeks. We teamed up after that.'

'Children can be such little demons.'

'Except Kishen,' I said, intending a compliment, but she didn't respond and looked sad instead of happy. Was her mother more attentive to him than to her, I wondered idly; he was so much younger, after all.

My mind, like a persistent fly, returned to the more pressing question of whether she would accept one of these suitors. No, probably not. But Champa was another matter—she would go back to her one of these days. My stomach contracted. Perhaps it was just hunger.

'Are you hungry?' I asked.

'I wasn't but the pakoras smell delicious. Come on, let's run.' She took off, and I had no chance against those long legs.

~

From the moment my eyes opened, I was waiting for her to appear in person or by proxy—for her footsteps coming down from the roof or her voice calling from the gallery next door. For one of her notes fastened to a jasmine garland and sent through Kishen, or folded like a paan and tucked into my sleeve in a crowded room. Or even waiting just to look through the window and see her leave with someone else. Often, I would neither see nor hear her. Instead, someone would mention that she had been seen somewhere.

'I saw Chapla in Machhi Bhawan with some man, I think it was Miyan Ma'aruf,' Chand remarked. 'Maybe he's trying to get to Azizan through her.'

'Or maybe he's transferred his affections,' laughed Shirin. 'If Azzo's not available, Chaplo will do. That's how men are.'

It was no laughing matter to me. I wanted to snap back that a hundred Azizans couldn't equal Chapla. But how could she spend time with that fool, Miyan Ma'aruf, who was neither wealthy nor witty nor good-looking?

The girls were well away now with jokes and puns, about kisses, *machhis*, stolen in the nooks and corners of the fort-like Machhi Bhawan. Fishes and kisses—curvy, slippery, wet. I forced my mind away from that delectable mouth.

How many times, just before dawn when everyone had finally fallen asleep, I'd risk climbing from our gallery onto theirs to linger near her door. The only sounds the harsh chinks and chirrups of squirrels waking to the battles of the day and birds opening their gambits. Was she stirring inside? Or away? Was someone with her? Her mother? Occasionally I'd leave a note, more often come away without a sign.

She might appear right away, or I might hear her voice in another room and I'd wonder whether to wait or to go in search of her. Usually, I'd get up and follow the sound of her voice. Once when I thought she was on her way, I lay on the divan, pretending to be asleep, hoping she would come in and bend over me, her regard for that one moment directed entirely towards me.

I strategized like a general organizing a battle, finding out her plans for the evening, and arranging to accidentally be exactly where she would be. But my plans were never bold enough.

'Didn't you think of getting me drunk some night?' she asked much later, laughing.

No, I never had. Strange that I, raised in our household, wasn't able to manage such a thing, or perhaps not so strange; I was a slow learner in these matters. After our late-night conversations, I sometimes persuaded her to stay in my room, though. 'You'll set all the dogs in the alleys barking if you go back now.'

'All right, but I hope Amma doesn't notice I'm missing.'

'You can leave at dawn.'

'If I wake on time.'

She blew out the flame, lay back beside me on the narrow divan and pulled the quilt over both of us. One of my arms was pinned between us, the other hand caressed her brow, cheeks, chin, then suddenly slid over her like a flashing blade I hadn't learnt to wield.

She sprang up; I ran into the gallery and halfway up the steps to the terrace, half-terrified, half pretending to be terrified, and she followed in a few moments to console and chide.

'All over the world,' she said meditatively, 'People are doing this.'

'What?'

'Advancing, retreating, making mistakes. Let's not meet for a couple of days. There's a song I must work on and get right.' She issued this mandate calmly.

But next day, she told her mother she'd be staying the night with me because we were writing a long verse epistle together. It was a pleasant game, writing couplets by turns.

'Let's show it to Mir Insha if he comes tomorrow,' I said, playing with her hair.

'We should work on it more first. Rangin Sahib has written one from a dancer to her friend turned rival. I don't think much of it, too stiff. What are you doing?' Most of our girls were given to constantly hugging and touching their friends but were wary of doing this with her because she was somewhat aloof. I was an exception and was making the most of it.

'Making a *nagin*,' I said, coiling an intricate knot above a plait, conscious of the word's double meaning—a female cobra, an enchantress who mates for life.

She leant back against me. I slowed my breath and willed my body not to quiver. 'I wish I had a sister. Yours is so different from you, though.'

'Yes. She's the pretty one and I'm the brainy one.'

'I don't know about that. I think you're nicer looking. Let's sleep on the floor, it'll be cooler.'

We spread several mats on the floor and lay an arm's width apart. Turning this way and that, I was trying to forget her proximity and go to sleep when suddenly she quoted the second line of one of Mir Insha's verses:

> *'Ji lootata hai par main majboor bebasi se'*
> You've stolen my heart but I'm powerless to act.

'Don't say any more now, leave it unsaid, go to sleep,' she added quickly when I began to remonstrate. Next morning, she was gone without explanation and I mooned around all day, by turns elated and dejected.

Mir Insha was greeted with cries of surprise when he arrived that evening. He had shaved off all his facial hair, even his eyebrows, and was enjoying creating a sensation. Would she come? Would she not come? There she was at the door. Would she stay or leave? She was threading her way to me.

'I thought I'd try looking an *azad* as well as being one,' he explained. 'Free from conventions, light as a feather, floating freely where I wish. *Qaid se donon jahaan ke yeh faqir azad hai.*'

'Hope he doesn't start wearing those awful asymmetrical pajamas the azads wear,' I whispered to her. The azads are Sufis of a sort, but they pride themselves on their liberty, breaking laws and rules of all kinds. Young men often join them for a season but drop out when they grow older. Poets are more likely to linger.

'Doesn't a poet need conventions?' Ammi asked him.

'Conventions don't make poets, poets make conventions,' he answered breezily, dropping down cross-legged on the cushions. 'Let's ask another poet. What do you think, Nafis Bai?'

I wasn't quite used to being addressed as a poet, so I fumbled for words, and Mir Rangin chimed in, 'True, true. You, for instance, are always inventing new ways of writing.' He bowed to Mir Insha, half-joking and half-serious. 'Poets and heroes, the free and the gallant, azads and *banka*s, don't care about conventions. Whatever they do becomes a new convention. Like Banka Begam, they set the style.'

'Banka Begam?'

'You haven't heard the story? He lived in Delhi at the time of emperor Mohammad Shah. Bands of robbers used to rove through the city, preying on the weak, robbing women of their jewels. One day he dressed up as a lady and sat in a palanquin, letting his arm hang out, covered with gold bangles.' She was idly playing with my bangles, moving two of them up and down. Could she feel the pores tingle, the fine hairs stir and rise? I kept my eyes fixed on Mir Rangin.

'When the robbers attacked, he sprang out and fought them; he killed several single-handed. The emperor called him to court and rewarded him. He went, dressed in his women's clothes, and after that, he always wore women's clothes and everyone called him Banka Begam.'

Mir Insha, never one to sit still for long, was moving around the room while the story was being told; he glanced through books and closed them, examined knick-knacks.

'He died fighting Nadir Shah's soldiers,' he put in now. A brief silence.

'We need more like him, especially on the roads between cities,' said Ammi. 'So many robberies and murders these days, even in broad daylight.'

Chapla dropped the bangles back and looked away as if thinking of something else.

Mir Insha decided to change the mood, throwing his head up and sniffing the air. 'What is this extraordinary scent? No, don't tell me, let me guess. Sandalwood, yes, but with a touch of, let's see, *bakul*? Well, Banarasi Bai Sahib?'

He turned enquiringly to Chapla who laughed and looked at her fingers. 'Yes, indeed, marvellous! I just mixed those two to perfume a fan.'

'I'm never wrong about smells,' he said complacently.

After everyone left, her mind was still running on Banka Begam. 'Men have all the adventures,' she remarked and stretched herself out with her head on my lap, while her agile toes tried to pick up my slippers. 'They get to fight battles, rule kingdoms and estates, and still wear women's clothes if they want to. I feel like a boy. I'm tall like a boy and my face is long, not round. Would you still have liked me if I were a boy?'

This was a tricky one—hard to imagine not being taken with her in any incarnation, but still harder to think of her without that body like a budding sapling, without that smoothest of smooth skins. I evaded the question by challenging the premise. I'd been drawing up my own lists.

'Women can have adventures and rule estates too,' I said. 'There's Ahalya Bai in Malwa, isn't there? She's been ruling for over twenty years now.'

'True. She's a greater builder than even your Nawab. She's rebuilt ever so many temples and ghats in Kashi.'

'Yes, and a couple in Ayodhya too. And there was Udham Bai, the tawaif who became emperor Muhammad Shah's third wife. Her son was the next emperor, Ahmad Shah Bahadur, and she controlled the whole empire for six years. And before her Lal Kunwar, another dancer who rose to be queen. Did you know, when she became queen, she made Zohra, a vegetable seller who was her closest friend from her dancing days, a noblewoman?' Greatly daring, I stroked her sleek, tightly pulled back hair which had just the slightest ripple in it, feeling at every stroke the shape of her head.

'Now everyone's talking about Farzana, that dancer from Kashmir. She rescued the emperor from rebels and she made a deal with the Sikh chieftain who conquered Delhi—what's his name?'

'Baghel Singh,' said Nadira, who had just come in.

'Baghel Singh. She leads her troops in battle herself, even though she's shorter than I am. The emperor calls her his dearest daughter.'

'She married a firangi, didn't she?'

'Yes, something like Samru I think his name is.'

'I've heard her best friend is a begam called Umda.'

'I wouldn't want to be her friend. I've heard she can't be trusted an inch and she's cruel. She whips her maids and tortures them.'

'Ratan was talking about Chanda Bai in Hyderabad,' Nadira put in. We had heard of her, but we sat up to hear more.

'He says she dances very well and also writes poetry, like our Bakhshi. They call her Mah Laqa Bai.' More moons! As if on cue, Chand came to the door. 'Chapla, Kishen is crying for you. He wants an ice *gola*, and Dadda says it's bad for his throat since he's been coughing.' Chapla leapt up and ran out.

I posed the original question to Sharad later. 'No,' he said decisively. 'You wouldn't have liked her in the same way if she were a boy.'

~

That was the year of marriage, at least in our lane; there were enough weddings to satisfy even Shirin. Our regular visitors, including the poets, had all been married off long ago. Mahtab Baji's patron, Khan Sahib, had produced twin sons with his one wife, and then made an art of avoiding the village altogether. Baji was tiring of him, though, because he was beginning to drink too much. Madanmohan now has two wives and five children; at that time, he had just one of each. Ratan's wife had died young and he hadn't remarried. Sharad was the only one who had never married. As a twelve-year-old he visited Hazrat Sahib in Delhi and there vowed not to marry. Which is not quite the same as a vow of celibacy, Mir Insha remarked, eyes dancing.

Men marry, often more than once, but they don't get excited about weddings the way most girls do. Other things excite them. The boys were full of gossip about the goings-on at the palace those few years before Mordaunt Sahib died. He was the Nawab's favourite and head of his bodyguards.

'What's so special about him?' I asked Sharad again, late one night. We were tired after a long session; the house was silent and dark. Everyone had eaten and gone to sleep. A lone candle flickered in my room.

'Come out here.' I stepped into the gallery. 'It's a bit cooler.'

'He's different, that's all. Everything about him—dress, voice, hair. He's very good looking, haven't you noticed? I find him a bit tiring but not everyone does. He's tall, slim, and what legs—perfectly turned as if on a lathe. His muscles flow like a robust river. Weren't you at that cock fight he hosted a few years ago, the one Zoffany Sahib is painting?'

'Yes, but I didn't think he was anything special. Mirza Hassan Raza was just as good looking. And he was with Nawab Sahib for years.'

'That's true, but he and Raja Tikait Rai were also inseparable, you know. Then they fell out with each other and Jhao Lal used the opportunity to get them both dismissed. Jhao Lal has the power now. Also, there's nothing like variety, and nothing so boring as the same body.'

I tried to imagine tiring of hers, and failed.

'Raza had put on weight and was languid; he lounges around, but Mordaunt's always on the go, killing something, hitting something, playing something. I'm not fond of watching hitting and killing, but Nawab Sahib admires it.

You should see Mordaunt with a pistol. He can hit twenty birds in the sky, with twenty shots, sometimes two together if they are flying athwart each other. He has a bullet lodged somewhere in his chest, but he thinks nothing of it.'

'How did that happen?'

'Someone shot him in a quarrel over a tennis game.'

'I heard he's virtually illiterate?'

'Yes, so was Raza, and what did that matter?'

'Nawab Sahib is a poet. How long can he be content with illiterate companions?'

'They're not his only companions. He has poets and scholars around too. Mordaunt is clever, and picks up languages fast. But desire seeks beauty, not scholarship. Why else would they all—Mirza Hassan Raza, Raja Tikait Rai, and Nawab Sahib - appoint dozens of useless but beautiful young men at court?'

'Including you now,' I teased.

He looked miffed. 'I'm overseeing the decoration of the new buildings. You'll see—he'll get his money's worth.'

Would Chapla mean as much to me if she were illiterate, I wondered. I had written out obscure Sufi poems for her and she had written out for me extracts from the Puranas and Kama Sutra, as she had promised. I had seen the Kama Sutra in Persian before, but this she wrote in Sanskrit with her own translations. As we talked, through long afternoons, about times and worlds, body and spirit, teachers and students, thoughts chased each other across her mobile features like clouds in the sky reflected in water. But what if her face had not been as striking as it was? My mind evaded the idea.

'Nawab Sahib spends a lot on Mordaunt?'

'Yes. His salary alone is three thousand a month. Can you imagine?'

Our kotha's monthly income was more than triple that, not counting the dry goods received, but I was too well-trained to reveal such secrets even to Sharad.

'I wonder what his parents think of all this?'

'Oh, they're far away, in England. And they say his mother is not his father's wife.'

'I see.' How many mothers are the wives of their children's fathers? My head teemed with the ones who were not—in our lanes, at the palace, and in the foreigners' homes.

'Anyway, he's making money hand over fist. Which parents would disapprove? He's built two houses. And spent a lot of time decorating them inside and out. One has an ornate garden with a sculptured well and fountain. Full of plants brought over from the Plowdens' place.'

'Well,' I yawned and stretched my arms above my head. 'The palace must be fun for you, with so many beautiful boys around.'

'At first, yes. But it gets tedious; most of them are empty-headed kids and all they can do is make dirty jokes which are funny only for a while. I'm going to Faizabad next month with Insha Sahib.'

'Ah, Ratan is there these days!'

I sensed his blush.

'You're attracted to him?'

'Almost everyone who knows him is, each in a different way. One as a mother, one a sister, one a friend, one . . .'

He hesitated. 'Like a firework you can't look away from though it's fallen on a bundle of hay.'

'I wish I could go with you.'

'Come, then.' He smiled. 'You won't leave while Chapla is here.'

He was right, though I did want to see Ratan dance and also perhaps catch a glimpse of Almas Ali Khan, who owned the largest estate in Awadh, and who Mir Insha said was truly a diamond.

'He's had an astonishing life,' Mir Insha had told us. 'He was captured in battle as a young boy, eleven or twelve, from a village in Haryana. And not just converted but castrated. That's how he became a khwajasarai. He could have turned bitter and mean. But look at him today—a great and pious man. Such a huge estate, and all the villagers on his land are his children, he says. He gives away a thousand rupees in charity every month. He's built a mosque and also a temple in his native village, where his Hindu relatives live. And the Begam Sahibas treat him like a son. They trust him with everything—the land, the accounts, the treasure, the keys. He's a gem, lives up to his name.'

'But what's the use, he can't have children,' piped Shirin who was always sure to interrupt with a parrot-like inanity just when one wanted to hear more.

'Any peasant can produce children, my dear,' replied Nadira. 'That's what Khala Jaan says.' True. Not everyone could earn Mir Insha's admiration.

I met Almas Ali briefly once, when he was a hale old man; I remember a wide smile, laughing eyes, long curly grey hair flowing on to his shoulders, the top of his head discreetly covered. Probably he never was fairy-faced, this nobleman and sage rolled into one.

~

First, Heera, my Dadda's daughter, married the sarangi player next door. This was no surprise; they'd been carrying on for a while. But then Mattan Apa's brother disappeared and after everyone had been searching for days, he showed up again with a flower-seller called Gori who was dark as night. His first wife, the quiet and somewhat whiny Dulari, threw a fit the likes of which none of us had ever encountered before, banging her head and screaming non-stop for hours. She calmed down only after Apa gave her a separate room.

The biggest wedding was Dulhan Jaan's. She was the setting sun of Mattan Apa's kotha, and became her long-time paramour's fourth wife when she decided to get pregnant. He was a trader in oils; the girls called him Oily Head, but they were thrilled anyway, especially Azizan. There would be a chance for a new planet to ascend, since Bakhshi was fading away. A tentative rapprochement between our houses began during the wedding preparations.

Tailoring clothes, preparing *ubtan*, weaving flowers went on all the time in our houses but now there was more than usual to do. Bangles from Jalesar, henna from Narnaul, *kajal* from Punjab, bracelets from Lahore, gauze from France, silks from Banaras and Mysore, wedding sheets from Chanderi. The girls had plenty to exclaim over and discuss.

Mir Insha wrote a poem about the wedding; he couldn't resist the opportunity to pun on Dulhan. He described it all—the bride's queenly ways and outspoken jests, the famous singers who congregated from far and near, the decorative ones amid the decorations:

Thousand-coloured fountains, sheets of water
In every corner, the fairy-faced cluster
Pearl garlands hang from ceilings
Emerald branches decorate doors
Door bolts studded with diamond fragments
Thresholds crusted with red rubies
Lamps glimmer like pearls of the night
Their light overflows, floods the darkness
Glass chandeliers enclose a garden
Fireworks crackle, sputter and spark

Chapla and I were in charge of the dramatic performances. Mattan Apa's kotha was much bigger and more opulent than ours, so there were plenty of spaces to choose from. A big central courtyard, with more than one level, plants and small trees in decorated pots lining it. The archways framing the galleries were more elaborately carved than ours, and there were more rooms tucked away behind the main ones.

We spent long afternoons rehearsing the girls in a comical piece about the Europeans carrying on—showering their necks with powder, having their servants carry chairs for them to picnics, getting drunk, turning red, and yelling in their own languages.

Azizan was a fair-skinned 'lady' who beat up her drunken husband while her young son, played by Kishen, monkeyed around. Shirin, put out at being assigned the part of lady's maid, found fault with every part of her costume and brought rehearsals to a standstill. 'This bodice is too tight under the arms and look how big the cups are, hanging loose. Our Mughalani is getting worse every day.' She tore it off and actually threw it at the poor old seamstress's head. But she missed, and it caught Ammi, who was coming through the door, right in the face. Chapla and I slipped out to the gallery to escape the ensuing fracas.

'I'm fed up,' I said crossly. 'They're all so easily distracted. Even Nadira keeps running off to do other things. And Kishen is too young to remember what he has to do.'

She put an arm round me. 'You're tired. Come here.' She drew me into my room, hand-fed me almond paste and rose syrup, made me lie down, and began massaging my temples with sandalwood oil. This felt unfamiliar; usually, I was the one to pet and feed and make much of her. The scent of her hair filled my lungs, as I closed my eyes. I turned my face into it, but just then, our seamstress came in, anklets clinking, with Chapla's bodice, which I had designed—white, covered with grape-trellises worked in silver.

While Chapla tried it on, Mughalani complained at length about Shirin, and I sat up to try and pacify her with paan. Azizan, playing ball in the gallery with Kishen, peeked in and threw the ball through the curtains to Chapla who was tying her bodice strings. It flew in on a slanting ray of sunlight, and she caught it with one hand, laughing, and adjusting her bodice with the other.

'How does it feel?' I asked.

'Pricks me,' she said, eyes dancing. 'It's too heavy with all this embroidery. Can't I have something simpler?'

I tossed her one of my own bodices, made of *shabnam*, called that because it's diaphanous as dew, sparingly embroidered with stars. 'Try this, then.' Oblivious, Mughalani commented, 'The stars will sink in that one.'

'Yes, both kinds of stars,' I said daringly, the blood rose to Chapla's face, and Azizan cackled with glee.

Rangin Sahib noticed we were both in white on the great day. 'This is too much,' he teased. 'You do everything together and now you also dress alike.' I tingled with pleasure at his pairing me with her. The festivities gave him material for his description of the wedding in his long romance about the Hindu princess of Kashmir and the Muslim prince of Bulgar. He produced a nice little vignette of our satires on the firangi sahibs with their liquor bottles and their Hindustani servants. Nor did he miss Chapla in a merchant's turban and my attempt to surprise her with an elaborate new hairstyle shaped like a lock and key, Chand in a waistcoat, quiet Bakhshi with her hair combed straight and simple down her back, and Shirin and Azizan with their loosely coiled tresses piled on their heads. Was he teasing when he suggested that she and I wearing white was a sign of our having lost desire for pleasure, or was he referring to Bakhshi again?

She who's a stylish beloved
Wraps her turban in many pleats

And she who has given her heart to *dogaana*
Designs a hairdo like a lock and key
She who considers all the rest shallow
Coils her hair up loosely
She who has no worldly ambition
Combs her hair down straight
The woman who's a player with friends
Is dressed in a waistcoat
She who's lost the desire for pleasure
Is dressed all in white

Surprisingly, he omitted Chand pouncing on Mahtab Baji in the bathing scene, perhaps because he didn't appreciate his inamorata's equanimity or perhaps because Ketaki Mausi had rebuked him about another poem he'd written characterizing various women in Banaras as firecrackers, tempests and riddles. We had got a round hole cut in a large mirror so that the girls looked as if they were in water. Chand, who was always chasing someone or other, took her chance. Mahtab Baji smiled sleepily and let herself be tussled. The scene went well, even Kishen remembered his part, but it was hard for me to take my eyes off Chapla long enough to focus on anything else. 'No man has ever gazed at me the way you do,' she remarked, half-flattered, half-flustered.

Apa's house was transformed. As we approached, we walked through gusts of fragrance—perfumed braziers but also the alluring aromas of food and wine. A host of servants I had never seen before swarmed around, lent for the occasion by one of Apa's old admirers from Sylhet, all of them wearing black dots on their foreheads to avert the evil eye.

After our performances, I wandered about, examining each transfigured room. Little touches everywhere—a concealed lamp, a crystal figure on a bracket, a small fountain. Her hand was on my arm, that slightly awkward yet possessive grasp. She drew me into a triangular corner room and we sat down in a window niche, looking out on a shaded part of the garden.

'So Dulhan Apa will be married, and in *parda*. I don't think I would like that.'

'It might be an easier life. Fewer people to please.' I answered as a parrot does, because I was looking at her, and drowning.

'Not necessarily fewer, just different people. Strangers. Will she ever sing or dance again?'

'Just for him, probably.'

She looked out of the window, thinking, and I at her. Don't go, don't go, my eyes cried out, cherishing her face. Don't go back to Kashi, ever. Stay here and dance for me. The words would not rise to my lips, though, for fear of being brushed off with a laugh.

The pleasure of being with her in a crowd was outdone only by the pleasure of being with her in my room (when we went to hers, it felt as if her mother was looking through the wall), telling each other stories, the endless stories of our lives before we met. Even now, the stories we told each other are more lucid to me than others, dyed in our telling of them. The lines she quoted to me and I to her unfold in me, still in bloom.

And poems—how many I wrote, some good, many bad. Never before or since have I written so many in such a short space of time. One spark setting off another, they flew between us.

I had plenty of time to work on them because she was often away, performing at various places, meeting various men—and women. I lived in a kind of red-hot daze, carrying on with my routine, not daring to plan or dream. Avoiding leaving the house lest she come over just when I had left. Standing outside her closed door for minutes that felt like hours, knocking, or failing to knock and retreating.

She wanted something too, but what?

What she wanted right now, apparently, was to cook for me.

'I'm going to feed you real Banarasi food. Not the heavy kind that your Nawabs and our Maharajas eat. Simple, gently spiced food that old Banarasi families prepare; it's *satvik*. You come and eat in my room tomorrow afternoon.'

But that first time everything went slightly wrong. The peas in the samosas were not fully cooked, the banana *kofta*s were too soft and fell apart, and the lotus seeds in the *sheer birunj* were a bit stale. I ate a little and made appreciative sounds but she could tell and was upset. It didn't help that Kishen kept sampling different dishes and then spitting out mouthfuls while pulling faces.

'I'll never cook for you again,' she said, pouting, as we sat together later after she had shooed Kishen out, and Nadira had carried him away to show him a new batch of baby chicks.

'Shush, it doesn't matter,' I said, rubbing perfumed oil into her scalp. We had each been given a bottle at the wedding along with many other gifts.

'Have you ever dipped your bodice in perfume?' she asked, stretching herself backwards cat-like.

'No.' It sounded most extravagant to me.

'You should try it some time. It feels wonderful. Wait, don't go, let's have some wine. I'm so tired from all that ridiculous cooking. I can't believe not one thing turned out right.'

'The beetroot and pea *puri*s were tasty. I like coloured puris.'

'Yes, but Amma made those.'

~

All this, yet nothing had happened. Nothing that anyone could name or notice. Champa came to visit—a pleasant, round face, a closeness to Chapla that it seemed I could never hope to match. Chapla took her to see the sights, while I decorously stayed home, wondering, imagining. Was I always to be on the outside of a closed door, in a separate room or at most on a bed two steps away from hers? Would others always have stronger claims on her? Was she just whiling idle hours away with me? If by some miracle she was indeed drawn to me, how long would it last? Would she stay? Would she leave?

One evening, Madan asked, 'Why don't you get out of here and see the world? Everyone but you seems to be constantly on the move.'

For the first time, I had been actually considering this possibility. 'Chand is going to Faizabad to visit an old friend of hers who's an attendant of Bahu Begam. I've never seen the palace there.'

'You must go. Enjoy yourself. Stop moping and waiting—what are you waiting for?'

What indeed? It was safe to go; Chapla was away on a long trip to Kalkatta and was going to meet Champa and others there.

The journey was easy, the palace magnificent. Though the company had robbed so much of the Begam Sahibs' wealth, they still had plenty to spare. Best of all, I didn't have to perform, I was not under scrutiny. One morning, Chand was sleeping late and I ventured out into the garden. Down a path edged by long, still dewy grass. Round a clump of trees and almost straight into someone who nearly tumbled me over.

'You walk fast!' A cheeky, dark face and a plethora of curls. She was shorter even than I was, buxom, easy to talk to, undaunting, and clearly impressed by me, the big city girl who consorted with poets. Her name was Maryam. Her mother was one of Nawab Begam's attendants.

'Do you like tamarind? I'll get some.' In an instant she was up a tree and sprang down, her hands full. She tasted one and pulled a face. 'Needs salt. Come to our place. My mother has gone to church.'

It was Sunday, to me like any other day. 'Why didn't you go?'

'I was asleep. I like to sleep late.'

The house was dark and low-ceilinged. I stood looking at the few books on a shelf, at a painting of the Virgin in a blue sari on a gold-starred background. She returned from the kitchen with a bowl of salt and chilli powder, I turned around, we almost collided again. 'This is meant to happen,' she said, chuckling, as we took one more step forward. Simple, pleasurable, no terrifying heights or depths. No one to observe us—her mother stayed at the palace all day, and Chand was otherwise occupied.

We had five days together, then I was back home, pleased with myself. Why torture myself over someone who seemed unattainable, when someone else was ready and willing? I knew why, but decided not to know for the moment.

No poems, but we wrote letters; we made plans to meet. I tried, unsuccessfully, to think only of Maryam.

Then, Chapla returned. For once, I had a tale to tell, and saw, with mingled fear and pleasure, her face darken like water when the sky clouds over.

4

It comes back to me in scenes, not so different from the way she comes back to me in dreams. Sharad frequents my dreams but not as much, usually inhabiting some odd version of the old house in his village.

An autumn evening—while waiting for the men to start drifting in, we went up to the roof just after *maghrib*. The pigeons had retired and could be heard stirring and murmuring. We sat on the low ledge and as I told her more about Maryam, the heavy golden moon made its way upwards. Behind us, the city glimmered. She listened with her usual sympathy, as if completely absorbed. Later, when I knew her better, I could tell when her mind was dividing itself, one part watching. Later, too, she told me that was the moment she knew it was only a matter of time. Now she knew she could lose me, knew too that I was not a virgin bold only in verse.

We drifted to the middle of the terrace, arms around each other, and our lips almost touched when Chand appeared at the top of the stairway and announced sardonically, 'Your guests are waiting for you', so we ran down the stairs, hand in hand, into the lamp-lit room and their amused gazes.

Shortly after Diwali she fell sick and, fleeing her mother's ministrations and Kishen's importunings, took refuge in my room. Her awkwardly graceful body rolled up in my quilt, her narrow forehead beaded with fever, her eyes shrinking into her fine-boned face.

As she recovered, the air cleared, the stars brightened, the first tinge of a chill appeared. Often, we sat up almost till dawn; that particular night she was showing me her mother's collection of old paintings. Only one light burnt as she unfolded the silk wrappings. We sat close together, heads bent over the delicate fabrics.

'Raga Bihag,' she said. A woman in mustard-gold and red on a flowered bed, shoulders bent backwards, arms stretched above her head as if awaking from sleep, another stepping towards her with a hand-mirror, and a third turning away to pick blossoms from a tree just outside the canopy. As we looked down at the picture, our fingers touched, entwined, sent lightning coursing up my arm, our hands opened, covered each other, closed, bone fierce against bone. A gust blew in from the gallery, set the little bells on the hookah tinkling, and the flame went out. In blessed darkness, we slid back on the divan against the wall, her lips travelled up my arm. Moonlight showed me her face, mouth half-open as if in agony. One instant suspended, then I grasped her face with both hands; her gasp as our mouths met and held goes through me like a shock as I write. The moon sent in its silver greyness, we talked meaninglessly about Maryam, about Champa, about the meaning of what we were doing, then fell back into kisses. I see it sharp as a carving, moonlit shadows slanting across the room, and her face bent over mine as we stood, clasped, in the familiar space that would never be the same again.

But was that our first kiss? 'I had a dream of you, of us together,' she wrote to me later, 'the night before I left here for home, the first time I visited your city. I'd gone over to see you the day after we met. You were wearing yellow. That night or rather early morning I dreamt of us together, of you in yellow. And just then you came to my door at dawn, remember? I was half-awake and somehow I knew, I opened the door, there you were, with the first sunbeam behind you. That was the moment, I think.'

What did I think or feel or do next day, until she came to me? A blank page. Nothing existed but the heat of her breath, the space between cloth and skin, daylight waiting for her voice, her step, her hands.

'Is Nadira really going this month?' she asked when she finally came through the curtains. As if one wedding were somehow connected to another. The space of the room divided us but now she crossed it without hesitation and laid her cheek against mine.

'Yes. It's so far away. And she knows no one there.' The words spoke themselves, then stopped. Her lips slid down my cheek to my throat, she breathed in sharply, words coming in spurts.

'You'll miss her. You've never been apart, have you?'

'Only for short periods. Do you miss the people in Kashi?' Avoiding Champa's name as I tore open her bodice fastenings.

'Yes.' But her looks were not rueful now as she put up a hand and drew the curtains, darkening the room.

Somewhat later, she took a small silver bottle out of her pocket, unstoppered it and poured perfume all over my bodice. 'There, I'll wring it out later and the whole room will be scented.' What would Dadda say about this waste, not to mention Shirin and Ammi and Heera and Nadira and everyone else who was always coming in and out? But I had not much time to worry about that because she was moving on to other things.

Her playful mood changed and finally she fell asleep in tears on my shoulder.

Next afternoon, it was my turn to cry. 'Sleep,' she said in the silent dark. And I slept.

~

This is what Bakhshi and Hazrat had meant then. The moment, when after toiling at a foreign language for months, it crystallises and forms pathways into a new world.

'Nafis, are you using a new lotion on your skin? You're glowing.' The usually unperceptive Mahtab Baji was smiling at me.

'No, not really,' I muttered, smiling back, my face growing warm.

As memory brightens, whitening moonlight, something tightens, condenses, throbs in me.

'We fall on each other like animals,' she said the second time we embraced. But we lacked the violent simplicity of animals. Fears, anxieties, forebodings muddied the water soon enough.

Maryam wrote, a letter full of endearments to say she was coming to town, and eager to see me. Champa was coming too. What did all this mean? I wrote back, a letter of lies and half-truths.

'Shall I try to put her off? Say I'm sick?' I asked.

'No, how can you do that?' she murmured. But later she followed me into the dressing-room.

'Tell her not to come.'

'How can I, now?' I parried, thinking, Can you stop Champa coming?

Would she leave me alone, I meant, alone and waiting, endlessly waiting? Could I stake everything on a mercurial girl who made no promises? Would she leave Champa, leave her friends, disappoint her mother just because she liked my poetry and the curve of my arms? Or even because she might be growing somewhat addicted to the hollow at the base of my throat where she had hung her flower-shaped, gem-studded *dhukdhuki* so that the pearl dangling from it beat at every pulse?

What would Sharad or Mir Insha have advised, had I asked them? I told no one though they may have guessed. *Prem na haat bikaaye*, she reminded me in one of her notes. But Kabir was speaking of the eternal. We live in the world's marketplace where a sale without witnesses is perhaps no sale at all. Though the price may be paid with every breath.

Maryam arrived. All I could see now was her crudity, and my body shut down as I went through the motions.

I closed my eyes to block out her face and saw another's, sometimes tear-streaked, when we met on the stairs, in a city garden, in the bathing room, when we passed notes to each other in books under Maryam's very eyes.

Sometimes, I lashed out at poor bewildered Maryam, criticising her clothes, her manners, her way of chewing cardamom, then embraced her to make up for my unkindness. She was my guest, staying in my room; Chapla saw me dress to take her out into the city, and thought that I had replaced one girl with another, just as I mistook her flirtations for fickleness.

Then came Champa. My fears descended like mists, cleared, descended again. They had grown up together. Like Nadira and me. 'We're like sisters,' Chapla had said. Who can compete with that? But when I left them together and went to bathe, Chapla appeared in the semi-darkness, pressed a note into my hand and her lips on mine.

I asked Dadda for milk last thing at night, pretending I had finally realized its virtues, dipped a new pen in it, and traced the letters carefully. 'Hold it over the lamp,' I murmured when I handed the note to her, over-written with one of Mir Taqi Sahib's ghazals in visible ink.

Milk, ink, blood. I seemed to have lost a layer of skin; I could feel blood pulsing close to the surface. Every inch of skin acutely awake, like lips, porous, easily cut, drinking in the air.

Desire ran mercury-like, from one edge to another, eluding the grasp, dividing, re-joining. I discovered how a trapped animal feels. Cajoling, being cajoled, and performing, always performing, for everyone around.

Subdued, all her bounciness gone, Maryam left, sooner than she had planned. Champa seemed cheerful enough; later, she said she had seen it right away. Soon after, Nadira married and went to Hyderabad. Everyone had wept and wailed, except Bakhshi and me, who should have cried the most. For one thing, I found it hard to cry in the presence of others. For another, now that my kernel of two had closed, I felt more like singing than crying. Bakhshi was too worn out by her continuous weeping, I suppose. Ratan went to Hyderabad a month later and met Nadira while he was there; he sent us her letters enclosed in his to Sharad. Unlike Chapla's, Nadira's followed the conventions of letter-writing we had been taught, and revealed little.

Every important observer was gone, and we blew together, dust settling after hot winds die down. The waiting had ended or rather I still waited but now with perfect confidence, as one waits for a pigeon to return home. One by one and two by two, her clothes both elaborate and simple, her flasks and vials, her books and pens, her peacock-shaped comb, her slippers, travelled into my room and dressing room. A few things, such as the little shrine of her Murali Manohar, remained in her room next door, to reassure her mother, and she sometimes slept there, but less and less often.

As a face, however sharp its lines, looks dew-soft when seen up close early in the morning, so edges softened, angles curved, harsh sounds sang. The cup fills but is never quite full, almost overflows, subsides, in each iridescent moment all the colours of earth and sky.

Kishen was our only witness, popping in at all hours. He had conversations with me that hinged on abiding themes. 'When I grow up,' he remarked gravely one morning, telling me about his playmates arranging their dolls' weddings, 'I'll marry a girl.' He paused. 'Or a boy.' Then, after a moment's thought, 'Or I won't get married.'

'You can see if you want to or not,' I replied, equally gravely.

'Yes, I have a lot of time to decide.'

'Sharu Mama is not married.'

'Not yet.'

I couldn't help laughing. 'You think he's going to get married?'

'He may be getting married right now.'

Chapla woke. 'Who's getting married, mouse?' She picked him up and squeezed him. He was already too heavy for me to lift but Chapla was used to it. 'Come on to the kitchen, it's breakfast time. I'm going to eat you up.' She carried him out, squealing and wriggling.

~

Sharad lying on a mattress on the floor in the room that was once Chapla's, next door. He remarks that my poetry is derivative, and of a kind that would become popular if I passed it around. My heart shrinks. Nadira comes in from the kitchen and argues with him. Now he's upset and goes to the mehfil where Shirin is singing. A number of people are sitting in groups, drinking milk with turmeric. I come in, sit next to him, and say, 'Chalo wapas.' He says, 'Chalo,' so we go to my room but begin to argue again.

5

Persian kittens were everywhere. Long-bodied and slender, their white silky fur trailing like royal robes, their unwinking eyes appraising and appealing, sapphire, emerald, agate. Looking across the room at an old mirror framed in topaz quartz studded with gems, I watched Chapla laughing in its milky depths. Sitting on the dark red carpet, she smiled down at the kitten walking slowly up her arm and batting at her long plait. Conscious of my eyes and perhaps of Plowden Sahiba's, she flushed slightly. She was fair enough for the blood to become visible, wine rising in a glass.

We had been asked to a ladies' get-together at Martin Sahib's house and here we were; Chapla had run into Plowden Sahiba at Polier Sahib's house, and then Plowden Sahiba—'Lizbeth' Chapla called her—invited her over to her own house to teach her some songs. Chapla didn't take me along there, I noticed.

The kitten's tail twitched; two pairs of golden eyes met like patches of sunlight in a glade touching and expanding. Did the kitten sense a being exquisite as itself? I fondled

Lizbeth's little boy, who was at the doll-like age, his hair feathery vermicelli, his skin thick cream. Kishen looked like him, but honey-hued.

'Won't you sing?' Lizbeth asked, tinkling on the harpsichord. She was collecting songs, and had already written down one of the Nawab's. Much later, I heard that she had them inscribed into a book, with paintings of singers, dancers, musicians. Did we two appear there, as we were that day, one in orange, the other in green?

We sat on the carpet and sang Abru Sahib's ghazal, which I had marked in the book I had given to Chapla that first morning:

Mil ga'in aapas mein do nazrein ek aalam ho gaya
Jo ki hona tha so kuchh aankhon mein baaham ho gaya

Jis tawajjoh par nazar kar jaan deta tha jahaan
So tawajjoh haa'i in aankhon se'in kyun kam ho gaya

Saath mere tere jo dukh tha so pyare aish tha
Jab se'in tu bichhra hai tab se'in aish sab ghum ho gaya

Raag ki khoobsoorati ke kooch ka dankaa bajaa
Jab gala [gila] mutarib ka yaaron seer se'in bam ho gaya

Two glances met and mingled, a world of loveliness was born
What was to happen happened between those meeting eyes
The world was charmed by the way those eyes met

Alas, why has that regard diminished in these eyes?
When we were together, dear boy, sorrow was pleasure
Since we parted, all my pleasures have vanished
Applaud the beauty of the melody's departure
When the singer's lament, friends, moves from treble to bass

Lizbeth clapped her hands in delight, and called her *munshi* to write down the words. I wondered where Sharad was right now, and Ratan. Had what was to happen happened?

Lizbeth and Chapla went on to the verandah to discuss the English king's fiftieth birthday celebration, at which Chapla was to dance. I sat with Jugnu and Zeenat, Polier Sahib's two wives whom he had left behind when he returned to Switzerland, and whom Martin Sahib had kindly taken in. They seemed cheerful rather than bereft, eager to chat and giggle as they made paan.

Chapla and Lizbeth came back, we sang a few more songs, then she and I slipped out into the garden. Which is more pleasurable—being alone together or being with others, knowing that the one they all desire will soon be alone with you?

They call the house Farhat Baksh now, after the Nawab bought it, but to me it will always be Lakh Pera. They certainly felt like a hundred thousand, those trees, whispering round us. We walked, entwined, down a narrow path, to the river slipping by. On the opposite bank, a few *jogin*s were exercising. Oiled muscles, tightly knotted hair, saffron *dhoti*s. A particularly sturdy one threw a discus. Abruptly, she turned to me, her arms tightened. Our toes pressed into the swimming earth. My eyes opened briefly, hers were dark points. Our only kiss in the open air.

For weeks, for months, I may not remember, and then all at once, all together, the scenes rise up, like paintings taken out after being hidden away, bright as if painted last evening, bright enough to hurt the eyes.

We walked back to the house, opened a side door and wandered through the rooms that housed Martin Sahib's collections. It was as if the contents of a dozen Chowks had been collected together in a shop redolent with cedar, bay leaves and cloves. Shimmering gauzes, velvets, muslins, silks—I could have clothed our whole establishment for decades of performances—coins, medals, jewels, paintings, mirrors, puppets, syringes, fishing rods, books, endless books in many languages, and machines I couldn't name, though I guessed some were musical instruments. Stuffed peacocks, parrots, monkeys frightening one as they loomed out of dark corners. In that whole fantastical collection, she was the most exotic, the one who held my eyes as she bent over glass cases, from which Burmese rubies and Rajputana emeralds cast unearthly gleams on her face.

'All their houses are like this, full of curious things,' she said. 'Martin, Plowden, Polier, Palmer, de Boigne.' She placed a large straw hat aslant on her head and struck various poses, mimicking each one's odd accent as she pronounced his name.

I stifled my laughter in my veil. 'Like the Nawab Sahib's museum.'

'Yes. Almost. He has the largest collection, I think.'

Gori Bibi, Martin Sahib's chief wife, called us out to the verandah to feed us. Two pomegranates on a silver dish—she picked out the ruby-red seeds and put them in small bowls for us. I was surprised when they melted in my mouth. She laughed.

'It's not a pomegranate, it's a sweet that looks like one. Our cook learnt the trick from Nawab Sahib's cook.'

'I've heard he can cook yams in a dozen ways?' asked Chapla.

'Oh, more, he can cook them differently every day for a month, and you wouldn't even know they're yams.' She poured out tiny cups of wine, scented with special roses from Martin Sahib's gardens at Najafgarh. She treated us like children and how old she seemed to me then, when everyone over twenty-five was in a category beyond counting. She's living with Martin Sahib's other women in Constantia now, where he lies entombed.

Gori Bibi took us up to the roof to see the hot-air balloon. It had carried a man into the sky. Risen above trees and hills as everyone does in dreams. A fortress the building was, with its moat, its drawbridge, its heavy iron doors, and here on the roof its turrets with slits for guards to shoot through. If all else failed, one could escape in the balloon. A tunnel through the sky. The barber who had nicked Nawab Sahib by mistake while cutting his hair, and whom Mordaunt had saved from execution, had been sent up in a balloon instead for punishment, and had descended safely about five miles away.

Then she took us all the way down to see the basement rooms that were partly submerged now. When the river receded during the hot months, they would drain and become cool spaces for Martin Sahib to live in. When we finally got into our boat, the house seemed to shimmer and drift, its top reaching up to the skies, its hidden depths below the river. The sun had not yet set but a full moon was rising amid a few scattered clouds. She sighed and lay down, her head on my lap, then pulled my orhni down so that it shielded both our faces from the sun's last flare. The boatman was facing the other way.

I was bending over her when someone hailed us, I started back, and there was Rangin Sahib, laughing and bowing. Mir Insha was gazing at the sky, his head on Rangin Sahib's lap as their boat drifted slowly past. He turned his head without raising it, and smiled at us knowingly.

'They've exchanged turbans, you know,' I said. 'They're brothers now. We should exchange orhnis.'

'Or bodices. But not transparent ones like yours,' she laughed, her fingertips, tender as lentil buds, travelling over my silk bodice and pressing the pearl buttons.

'Those two are on the rise,' she said. 'Now that they've joined the court of prince Sulaiman Shukoh.'

'Yes. As soon as he moved here from Delhi, they were introduced to him because of their friendship with his brother.'

'The one who just died?'

'Yes. But that's not the big news for Rangin Sahib. The big news is that Mahtab Baji has decided to take him after all, since he's prospering. She's shown Khan Sahib the door.'

'Really? A happy conclusion for Rangin Sahib, after all that drama.'

Later that night, when we were all sitting together, Mir Insha remarked, 'What a lustrous evening. It inspired a new ghazal.'

'Please let us hear it,' said Ammi politely, and he launched into it right away, still smiling at me.

Chaudahvin taarikh ik abra tanik sa tha jo raat
Sahan gulshan mein ajaayab sair mein dekha tha

Jhilmili si chaadar mahtaab oopar barq ka
Voh dupatta baadle ka tha, jo lahraaya kiya

Yun laga maalum hoti hain ye do pariyaan baaham
Ek ne goya ki saaya doosri par aa kiya

Bu-e gul boli ki aaj aapas mein badli orhni
Chandni khanam ne bi chapla se behnaapa kiya

Khud badaulat to na aa'e aur Insha raat bhar
Aap bin roya kiya, lota kiya, tarpa kiya

On full moon night a small cloud arose
Out in the flower garden, I saw a wonder

A shimmering veil of lightning over the moon
A cloudy veil of fine fabric fluttering

They seemed to me two fairies close together
One drew near, cast her shadow over the other

Flowers' perfume said they've exchanged veils today
Lady Moonlight has become Lady Lightning's sister

You didn't have the grace to come, and Insha all night long
Wept, writhed, throbbed alone, without you

Pari, they call us, and for the first time I felt fairy-like, caught in the magical circle of light cast by his verse. As they applauded, several listeners smiled and looked at us.

Next morning, she rehearsed with Azizan, and then we lay in her room eating litchis. I peeled and put them in her mouth one by one as she reclined on a bolster, and she playfully spat out the seeds, aiming for the window. One of the musicians yelled from the street downstairs, demanding to know who was being so rude. Between pretend-scolding and laughing, I asked idly if her name meant anything besides lightning.

'It has many meanings. It's one of Lakshmi's names—she doesn't stay long in one place, you know. She's called Chanchal, the restless, the playful one. And it means fickleness, mischief, wine, the tongue.' She stuck hers, unusually pliant, out at me, then leaned forward to transfer a litchi to mine, and the warning slid away like juice down my throat.

That was the only winter I had something to do with the Christians' Big Day, the birthday of Jesus. Chapla was taken with the idea of doing something to mark the day. I should have wondered how Maryam was doing, today of all days, but she had disappeared from my mind as a small cloud melts into a flawless sky. Plowden Sahiba had left for Kalkatta a few weeks earlier, so we went to the Palmers' house, where Chapla had once performed. We knew one of their maids, who took us to her room and gave us that black cake with nuts that I don't like but that everyone else adores.

I scarcely remember the visit but I remember returning along green lanes through a sunlit winter haze. She was sometimes ahead of me, sometimes behind; we floated and bobbed, two kites playing in the breeze, touching, drifting, then touching again. When we got back, the others were sleeping late as we were not working that evening. She wanted to try making a sweet dish she had seen made in firangis' kitchens. It had to be steamed in a greased bowl. We mixed milk, butter, sugar, then crumbled bread, nuts and raisins into the mixture. In the liquid our fingertips touched, pressed. She raised hers dripping and put them between my lips.

'Delicious,' I said, sucking, and then pulled her down to the coal-stained floor.

'There's water on the fire for a second pudding,' she protested weakly. 'I overfilled the pot, it'll boil over.'

'Let it.'

'We should cook more often,' she said later, laughing, after the water had boiled over and the pot was scorched. 'Seems to inspire you.'

Those few months of being together day after day are a fixed, unmoving circle of light. I remember only a few special days. Is that what happiness is—the cessation of happenings? It was winter but felt warm, waking every afternoon cushioned in rose petals, and going to bed in the last reaches of the night cradled in velvet.

Madan was the only person I told. Pleased to be singled out as my confidant, he took us out to an inn. This was a new enjoyment to me; she had stopped at inns for meals on her many travels. He obtained a private room. In the open pavilion overlooking the river, men gathered, two female singers from a kotha less prominent than ours sang, and a dancing boy performed, all of them stopping at intervals to puff on a hookah. Our room too had a view of the river. Bare-chested servers ran in and out, with hot breads of various kinds. The food was interesting, spicier and greasier than we were used to.

Madan beamed benevolently on us. She got up to visit the bathroom, and I accompanied her. As we closed the door behind us, I daringly blew out the candle and pulled her around to face me in the sudden darkness.

Early morning on Holi, I couldn't find her anywhere. Heera found me first and soaked me in the orange of palasa flowers. With a pitcher of red hibiscus water, I went next door, saw Ketaki Mausi embracing Ammi and asked her where Chapla was. 'Haven't seen her, bitiya. Go look in her room.'

I looked into all the rooms but they were empty. Everyone was outside, screaming and getting drenched, some in the backyards, some in the back alleys. A troupe of revellers in costume came in from the alley. One in a saffron sari, no bodice, barefoot, bare-armed. That hair cascading like a waterfall gave her away even before I saw her face. 'Look, look, Heera,' I pointed over the many intervening heads. 'Look at my *gu'iyaan*.' In my excitement, I said it, but perhaps no one heard, amidst the screams. Many others were looking too, all the free-eyed, freethinking men, young and old. Why is open hair so enticing?

The house rang with screams and laughter, then subsided into torpor as we bathed and then retreated, tired, to our rooms. But her mischievous mood lingered. In my dressing room she stood, her back to me, draped in a long and heavy violet veil, edged and spangled with gold, while I pulled on a *lehnga* to be comfortable.

'Just hold up a mirror for me to see how this looks,' she said. There was never any shortage of mirrors in our houses. I picked up a rectangular hand-mirror, then gasped as she half-turned, clad only in strings of pearls, emeralds and rubies.

In the late afternoon, Mir Insha dropped in, on his way to the evening festivities at the palace. He was in a luxurious marigold-coloured outfit, all aglitter. 'You and I look alike,' he teased her, eyes sparkling with mischief. 'I was a fairy-faced one in my youth, believe it or not, Chapla Bai.'

'Oh, I believe it. You're still beautiful, Masha'allah.'

Immediately after Holi, the city began preparing for the English King's fiftieth birthday. Rumour had it he was going crazy but that didn't affect the celebrations. Flower-sellers, jewellers, clothiers, shoemakers, tent-makers, *halwai*s, oil-sellers and all the other kinds of traders and artisans had more work than they could handle. I was in charge of our group's costumes, especially hers for her big debut at the Residency. I combined green satin pajamas with light-blue silver-edged silk gauze for her peshwaz, and was sitting with Ram Awadh the jeweller, holding Kashmiri sapphires against them, when Mir Insha and Sharad walked in.

'You're turning her into earth and sky, are you, Chandni Khanam?' Mir Insha teased, playfully draping the dupatta, light as a cloud, covered with moon and star-shaped spangles, over his head. 'Ah, the smell of unworn cloth, there's nothing like it. This French gauze smells of the mountain brook they washed it in. It is French, isn't it?'

'Yes, so Motilal-ji says. Will you write an ode for the occasion, Mir Sahib?' I asked.

'I will, and I'll make your young lady a star in the firmament, wait and see. A dancer dances just once, but a poem lives forever.'

'Or as long as it's remembered,' said Sharad sombrely, getting up to leave but lingering.

'Blue sapphires are inauspicious,' pronounced Mir Insha, touching them in my hand.

'No, no, that's a foolish idea.' Ram Awadh was displeased by this interference with a potential sale. 'The English say it tests a woman's loyalty.'

I dropped the sapphires.

'Turquoise or amethyst?' I held up two strands.

'Turquoise.' Sharad may delay big choices but not small ones. 'I really must go now. See you tomorrow.'

'She already has pearls. And they will go with those colours. Like the milky way or like a river,' said Mir

Insha. 'She's from Banaras. But Ganga won't do.' He was following a thought. 'It's Jamuna that's the river of passion.'

'Because Radha and Krishna played on its banks,' I put in.

'No, no, *pyari*, you're too busy thinking of union these days. But separation—separation is the real thing. Ever heard of the *chakva* and *chakvi* who long to meet at night? They're separated by river Jamuna. You're an innocent; you know nothing about passion.'

I smiled to myself but it didn't escape him. 'You don't. You think you do, but you don't. To know how powerful something is, one must first lose it.'

He returned to the original topic. 'It's a festival of the foreigners. Shouldn't you get her something new-fangled, something firang?'

Ram Awadh spread out a variety of trinkets. I picked up a Portuguese heart-shaped gold-filigree pendant, then my eye fell on a ring. Rings had been on my mind for a while. This one had a tiny watch embedded in pearls, diamonds and rubies.

'It's from Switzerland, bitiya, Polier Sahib's land, you know,' Ram Awadh informed me. 'They make the best watches. It will last a lifetime. And it's the only one—no jeweller in the city has anything like it.'

A lifetime. The only one. I had to have it.

'Set it aside. I'll pay for it separately.' No need to hesitate now about buying things for her.

Mir Insha was captivated. 'Perfect. A modern ring-watch for a modern girl. I must put in a line about it.'

And he did. He described every detail and transferred others' emotions to himself as he had to for the sake of the poem.

Sharad, however, didn't approve when I showed it to him next evening. 'I met a Chinese man in Delhi,' he said, 'who told me that giving someone a watch means time is running out.' I decided to disregard this, telling myself that time is always running in any case.

'Oh, and another piece of news, my dear,' he added, reclining on the divan. 'The Nawab has acquired Zoffany Sahib's painting of Mordaunt Sahib's cock-fight. You remember, you were there?'

'Yes.' I remembered sitting behind the others, to avoid seeing the cocks tear into each other.

'He's done two or three paintings of the same subject, it seems, almost identical but with slight differences. Anyway, your mother is there in pink, and Mahtab Bai, and you too, maybe.'

'No, really?' Chapla came in and heard the last bit. I tucked the ring-watch into my bodice where it beat as if in tandem with my heart.

'Yes, Mahtab Bai is in golden yellow and is reaching out for water. Nafis and Nadira are in the background.'

'This I must see,' said Chapla. 'How exciting!' She shot me one of her sidelong smiles.

'Don't expect too much.' Sharu was never one to flatter. 'He's made Nadira look round and goggle-eyed, and Nafis as usual is like a mouse hiding near her mother. But I'll show it to you. Tell me when you can come and I'll arrange it. So, Chapla Bai, are you ready for the big day? Many gentlemen are madly eager to see you dance. That gathering at Mir Rangin's house was the talk of the town.'

Chapla gave him one of her equivocal smiles. 'What do you think of these shoes? Nafis designed them.'

'They're wonderful—those pearls on the creamy gold and white form a nice contrast with the red heels. Like feet with *alta*.' Sharu was a good judge of dress, so I was pleased with his admiration of my skills if not my person.

Late at night before the big occasion, I tried the outfit on her; the fabrics I had chosen kissed her skin, her skin not washed-out white like the English ladies' but *kanak kamini*, warm as wheat, as gold.

'Like lightning flashing in the summer sky,' I said, as I tied the silver drawstring with its pearl pendants, gleaming through the pale blue swirl of the peshwaz and dangling below its hem.

While I dressed her she undressed me, discarding the purple I had selected for myself.

'Purple doesn't suit you,' she said. 'Parrot-green blossoms on you. Wear this green one with—let's see.' She threw her red orhni over me. 'There—it's like a flame on you.'

Until then purple had been my favourite colour. I've never worn it with pleasure since.

The night sparkled and so did all of us, lit by the sheen of youth. Even I felt beautiful when her eyes touched me. The whole town seemed to be there, troops of merchants with tributes for the English, foreigners with heavily powdered hair, and every dancer worth the name. Bands were playing foreign instruments, organs bellowed and fireworks fizzed above. A group of hijras performed and then Ratan. I looked up from a dark corner where I was adjusting Chapla's shoes with their long curling toes, to see Sharad framed in a lighted doorway, chest half-visible through lacy white embroidery—a flowering tree covered with leaves and buds. His hair was abundant in those days, long curls almost out of control, and his eyes were on Ratan.

Mir Insha was in his element—flitting from group to group, alight with laughter. 'Even the buds are proffering their glasses,' he whispered to me, as champagne bubbled up in crystal for a fat European lady and her young daughter. 'Look, flowers and bunches, all are imbibing.' I giggled; the lady's dress, billowing stiffly round her, did make her look a bit like a bunch of large showy flowers, the kind that the white people favour.

Then he whispered to Chapla:

Chaar naachaar hu'a jaana hi Landan apna
Le ga'i chheen ke dil ek firangan apna

No choice, I have to go to London now
A foreign woman has snatched away my heart

At this, both of us burst out laughing and Ammi threw us a reproachful glance.

He brought it all to life again in his poem—glasses, bottles, free-flowing liquor, lights in the trees, delicacies laid out on tables. He ignored Azizan resplendent in magenta and gold, and devoted his attention to Chapla, doing justice to my handiwork:

With a silken drawstring flowing like water,
Satin trousers blooming like foliage,
A light blue silk peshwaz like a cloud,
Its skirt edged with silver like a moonflower,
A veil of moon and stars like a moonlit night,
Anklets tinkling like drops of rain,
Chapla Bai stood up to dance.
Seeing her, Khutan gazelles forget to leap
Nature made her replete with beauty
From her face the Pleiades borrow radiance
The envy of fairies, she's called 'Lightning'
Light's world turns dark when she departs . . .
Who can praise the breasts of that infidel idol?
Oh lord, their curves and that rising youth—
Half-blossomed lotuses, two fine founts,
They shine like round swelling whirlpools
Or like chakva and chakvi sitting on two shores,
The string of pearls between is Jamuna . . .
That ring-watch blooming with delicacy
I'd sacrifice to it hundreds of sounding organs . . .
Her plait like the shade of a *kadamb* tree . . .

What an eye he had for detail—the verse I liked best described how her red heels made the white beads on her pearlescent white silk shoes reddish like *ratti*, those poisonous seeds used to weigh gold, or like red *champa* flowers with their creamy insides:

Those two arms boughs of the tree of Paradise—
Obtain from them what your heart desires

Her forearms male and female skinks
The sight of them drives men and women wild . . .
Those red heels make the pearls on her shoes
Look like red ratti seeds or champa flowers
. . . Today's the fourth day of the month of June
This happy day shines with special beauty

That night, the boughs of the paradisal tree caught me, pushed me down on a table, and the Jamuna flowed all over me. Now a maiden bereft of clothing, now the youth clasping her under a blossoming kadamb tree, I forgot daybreak nearing, and rejoiced when she snuffed out the flame.

Summer was at its height, and she sat behind me on the cool floor, arms wrapped around me, hair streaming over me, as we sang Rangin Sahib's new ghazal, in which a girl sang to a girl, and which we had made our special song:

Zanakhi ki rangat-e jawaan o peer soney ki
Saraapa voh nazar aati hai ik tasveer soney ki

Kinaari gird yun chehrey ki us ki zeb deti hai
Musawwir jo kahti hai tasveer ki tahreer soney ki

Galey ke haar tẹre ho rahi hoon a'e lagga main
Nahin darkaar tujh ko jaan-e man zanjeer soney ki

My dearest has a youthful complexion, like yellow gold
From head to foot, she looks like a picture of gold

Her scarf's border frames and adorns her face
Her words shaped like calligraphy on a picture of gold

I've become the necklace round your neck, dear one,
So, my life, you don't need a chain of gold

Summer brought less pleasant things too, like insects. One evening, a large cockroach came flying through the open window and circled my room. I screamed and hid in the dressing room, calling for someone to kill it. Chapla calmly took a cloth and drove it back out of the window. 'It's only a small insect,' she said.

'I hate them,' I retorted. 'There are thousands of them—wasps, bed bugs, flies. Have you read Mir Insha's satirical odes to them?' 'No, you must show me.' She seemed somewhat weary.

Now her many moods were all for me. When she picked a fight and went away to her room to sulk, leaving me in despair, only to send a contrite note over and follow it next day. When she pranced around, mimicking Mattan Apa's complaining voice, Mahtab's slow movements, and the clumsy manouevres of Ma'aruf Miyan with Azizan, sending me into peals of laughter.

When we both burst into uncontrollable giggles as he lugubriously recited one of his dreary ghazals, making eyes at Azizan all the while. Ammi gave us a stern look and then returned her gaze to him. Everyone else managed to keep a straight face but for some reason she and I, sitting together, kept setting each other off without even exchanging glances.

When we talked about dreams and the philosophers who say that life is a dream from which we will wake up. Champa, she told me, could direct her dreams, could pick up and continue a dream she had had the night before.

'If we could all do that, would there be no difference between a dream and life?'

She smiled wryly. 'Only if we all had the same dream.'

When she sat working on her poems, puffing at the hookah. Our verses answered, completed each other, played on each other's names, hidden codes we thought only we could decipher. Two nutshells concealing a joint kernel, twinned buds on one stem. Milk and saffron, colour in every drop.

Or when I started up from our bed, hearing footsteps, and ran into the dressing room with her purple veil draped across my chest and she followed, murmuring, 'It looks like a coal cellar on you. Take it off. What do you want with an orhni anyway except to cover your head—a little thing like you?'

'I want to smell it,' I teased, holding it over my face and then dropping it to the floor and her on to it.

When we argued over mangoes, an argument one can be sure of hearing in every home every summer.

'Kashi's mangoes are much sweeter,' she said, eyes dancing at me over the green-skinned one she was devouring. 'Like honey. Golden. And not stringy at all.'

'They're too sweet,' I said. 'Ours have a dash of sourness to set off the sweet.'

'Langras are rounder; they fit nicely into your hand.'

'You seem to be doing pretty well, fitting ours into your hand.'

'That's because I'm good at it. Watch.' She picked up another and slowly began pressing a thumb and two fingers upwards from its base to its peak, her eyes transfixing mine. When she pinched off the end and began sucking, her wide mouth half-smiling through the juices, I was thankful I'm not fair enough for a flush to be noticed. Though everyone else squatting round the bucket was too absorbed to care. The children had pounced on the basket the moment it arrived from Dashehri. Dadda could hardly restrain them until she had soaked the mangoes long enough to satisfy herself of their edibility.

Practice, which takes up the best part of our waking hours before the evening, and which, like most work, is sometimes painful, sometimes pleasurable, often tedious, now became a joy when I managed to slip away next door or when she came over to our place. As I sang, I could continuously watch without subterfuge her flexile face and body that I knew so well yet that seemed ever-new, or sit next to her to watch others. That inch of space between us warm as the space between two parted lips. Often, though, I had to help out in the house while she was practising next door and this was difficult, because I couldn't stop imagining her, and wondering when I could get away, when she would finish for the day, when we could meet.

Stolen wine is sweet, the poets say. I had never drunk so deep before. Lifting the latch of her door in the hour before sunrise, like a parched wanderer in the desert. Embracing on the stairway, amid mingled sounds of revelry and domesticity. Kneeling before her and then jumping up to rearrange our clothes at the sound of Dadda's footsteps on the stairs. No one was deceived, I realized later. They went along with our masquerade, perhaps not deeming it important enough to interrupt.

Important—was that the right word? What was the word I wanted? One afternoon, as she rested from her labours, I was chopping *supari* with my mother's old brass cutter, shaped like a pair of mermaids. Their curly heads nestled together, their fish-tails curved apart, and their centres met repeatedly as the mound of slivers below grew. I picked up a nut and found it was a doubled one. A flesh-coloured almost-heart resting on my palm. I imagined the flower shapes conjoined within. Did I dare give it to her? If a woman offers a dogaana or doubled fruit or nut to another and she takes it in her right hand, the two of them become dogaana or doubles, and announce it by distributing fruits or nuts of that kind to everyone they know. But if she takes it in her left hand and says, 'I remember,' no proclamation takes place. Would she take it in her right hand, on purpose or by mistake? If she did, in an instant our private melding would become public. She would distribute hundreds of suparis, superior ones from the Dakkan, to everyone in our lane. She was my other self, but would this ever be known and celebrated?

Suppressing the tremor in my hand, I held the doubled nut out to her, not meeting her eyes. She laughed lightly and took it with her left hand, saying, 'I remember.' So much for that. I chose not to think of her refusal, dwelling instead on her caressing voice that promised so much.

Just then we heard Sharu in the gallery, announcing, 'De Boigne Sahib is going to marry Noor Begam.'

This was news indeed and allowed us to get over the moment of awkwardness by going to join the hubbub. Noor Begam was the daughter of a general in the Mughal army, and belonged to a noble family. But she was a widow and lived with her sister, Faiz, who had married Palmer Sahib. Everyone surrounded Sharu, and ventured an opinion.

'Who but a firang would marry her? Once that sister of hers married Palmer Sahib, she was done for.'

'Let's hope he doesn't leave her and go back to his own land, the way Polier Sahib did.'

We soon found out that the wedding was to take place in Delhi. There were to be many feasts, and Azizan, Chapla, Shirin, Chand, were all to perform.

She still travelled constantly, and when I try to add up the days we were together I think it was only a few months after nearly two years hovering on the edge. But it seemed that she had stopped searching and I lived in a halo-like stasis.

The rains began but it was so sultry between downpours that most of us couldn't resist sleeping on the rooftop. After getting drenched two nights in one week, all of us returned, complaining, to our rooms.

We were adept at finding ways to escape everyone's eyes. 'Let's go back to the roof?' she proposed one night, breaking reluctantly from me as Dadda's footsteps approached down the gallery.

'What if it rains again?'

'It won't rain much, maybe just a few drops. Look, the clouds are scattering and the moon is rising.' She threw open the window and quoted Insha Sahib.

Charh ke kothe dhoop mein tum to uraati ho patang
A'e dogaana chandni mein yaan ura jaata hai rang
Pighli chandi ki tarah se hai thilakti chandni
Aaj kothe par laga do merey soney ka palang
Dogaana, you climb to the rooftop in the sun, and fly kites
While my colour fades even in moonlight
The moonlight quivers like melted silver
Lay my bed of gold on the rooftop tonight

'We're already on the kotha,' I said, laughing. 'Besides, that poem doesn't suit us at all. You're the one who flies kites and you're also the one with the moon-complexion.'

'You're so literal-minded.' She stretched and yawned. 'Of course it suits us—your skin is like golden silk—' She ran her fingers down the back of my neck and I caught my breath, '—and we are the ones with the bed of gold. We are Ganga and Jamuna meeting.' She laid her fingers aslant over my mouth; their coolness scorched my lips. 'Now don't say that it should be Ganga and Gomti.'

When we reached the roof, and lay down, I saw she had brought a wine goblet with her. She poured some straight into her mouth, leaned over, and trickled it into mine.

Was that our last moonlit night together? The last that I remember. We lay, tossing plans and fantasies back and forth, while the moon scurried between rusty clouds, now covering his face, now revealing it.

'If only we could create something new,' she said. 'Now that both Dulhan Jaan and Nadira have gone and Shirin is on her way out too, it would make sense for you to join forces with Mattan Apa and I could move here.'

I sat up. 'What a good idea. And we could maybe buy up the small house in between, where you're living. You can move into Nadira's room. We can write more songs together for you and Azizan to dance to.'

'You'll teach me Farsi.'

'And you'll teach me Sanskrit.'

'Gori can have the shed in your back yard.'

'Will Mausi agree to move?'

'I don't know. None of them may agree.'

'Or maybe you could move here on your own?'

'Maybe.' I sank back, her arms over and under me feeling not like a prison but like home long sought. 'I want a home with you,' she said. 'So that wherever I go, you'll be waiting for me when I come back.'

In Delhi the next round of disasters was beginning. That rainy season emperor Ali Gauhar was blinded by his favourite turned traitor, Ghulam Qadir. Dadda, who had raised Ammi in Delhi and had seen the emperor many times, came rushing up to the roof where I was watching the others fly kites. She was weeping wildly and when she began talking of blinding, I almost thought she had gone crazy and was reliving the days of her youth when Imad ul-Mulk had blinded emperor Ahmad Shah. Hard to believe it had happened all over again. I have an unfortunate penchant for physically reacting to the idea of pain; my eyes burned and winced. Ammi said nothing but looked pensive, remembering her putative father perhaps. Azizan began to cry, more because Dadda was crying than anything else. Chapla put an arm round her and made her sit down. She was always sweet to the younger ones and good with children.

'Thank God you all moved when you did,' Mahtab Baji remarked. She was a local girl who had joined the kotha when my mother moved here. 'Shahjahanabad is such a dangerous place.'

Ammi took the bait. 'As if there are no dangers here. It's all because of that wretched khwajasarai Ghulam Qadir—he was trouble from the start. And it seems the other khwajasarai who was in charge of the women's quarters let him in there to torture the women.'

'Oh, Ammi. What has being a khwajasarai got to do with it? Look at Mir Almas Ali, the English got him tortured but he wouldn't tell them where the Begams' treasures are.'

'Hastings Sahib is paying for that now, I hope,' Chapla said. 'His trial has started in England, I heard at court.'

Ammi had no answer so she responded as older people usually do. 'All right, girls, go and do something else—have you no work, nothing to rehearse? Children these days—always sticking their noses into their elders' affairs.'

Kishen was all ears and later said to me sombrely, 'Many people died in Delhi. When my Amma dies I'll stand in front of a carriage that is running very fast.'

Taken aback, I asked, 'Why?'

'Because I want to get hit.' The body in the chariot and the eternal self in the body, I thought but didn't say.

'Shush. Come on, let's go and feed the pigeons.'

In the lazy winter sunshine, they clustered round us, demanding grain.

'We're returning to Banaras after Holi,' she said, not looking at me as she pushed a grain through the dust with one toe. 'But I'll come back next winter and before that I'll see you in Delhi at Noor Begam's wedding.'

Here it was, the day long dreaded and denied.

'Such a long time?' My voice remained steady. 'Kishen, don't go so near the edge of the roof. Remember how that boy Lakhi in the next lane was walking backwards on the roof flying a kite, and he tumbled off and died?'

'You can come and see me any time before then. But perhaps you'll forget all about me.'

'What nonsense.'

'Perhaps you'll take up with someone else? Some Mogra or Chameli or Zeenat? Yes, a Zeenat, I think. You'll ask her over, feed her kheer and kulfi, and show her your poems.'

Her head dropped to my shoulder, like a lotus closing at night. Her teasing didn't trouble me. The illusion of completion had me in its hold, the mirage of bodies and minds melding, water and air.

Perhaps the dissolving began on the day we went to Aathon ka Mela, the fair at the Shitala Devi temple, which Raja Tikait Rai had rebuilt when someone found the *murti* of the Goddess in a nearby pond. He had built a magnificent tank too.

Our second Holi together. She was briefly back between trips. As she applied kajal, and I was putting on the sari she had brought me from Kashi, its starched folds resisting my fingers and spilling over the floor, she asked, as if forcing out the words, 'Would you move to Kashi?'

Taken by surprise, I laughed aloud. 'Kashi? Me? How can I?'

As I said it, I saw the morass I had stepped into. It must have taken her a long time to frame the question. Her face hardened and she turned away.

She rapidly descended the stairs, and I stumbled after, holding up the stiff sari, pleading, trying to take back my words. Fear settled in my stomach, the fear that was always dripping, quietly, behind the onward rush of joy, a small but persistent leak hidden in a wall. She relaxed in the palanquin and let me hold her hand, but a briefly opened window had half-closed. My misery simmered at the fair, thickened by the newly wed couples crowding to the temple, and by Azizan and Heera's presence, which prevented us from talking.

While she was helping them choose bangles I moved away, thinking. Was there a city that could belong to both of us? Delhi, perhaps? I walked through the heavy fragrance under bakul trees, among thousands of tiny blossoms littering the ground. Trying not to step on any, I started picking them up. Little crowns, each in its petal frill. Each like a star opening up, bent backwards as if in ecstasy, to reveal a creamy ring and a peak, tear-shaped, at its heart. I bought a needle from a stall and sat on the steps to the tank, stringing them together.

'Madhugandha,' she said, when I fastened the garland round her plait, and we went home, tranquil. But later it seemed to me that all our discussions about how to manage the separation and move to one place were haunted by my first spontaneous response.

In the end, I never did go to Kashi. Sometimes I feigned sickness, but mostly because my job was to handle all our affairs here, I claimed that the establishment couldn't carry on without me. I must be the only one in our lane who hasn't been to Kashi.

She was away in Faizabad when late one afternoon Mahtab Baji came running in. When Mahtab Baji ran you could be sure something was seriously amiss. 'Come quickly, Bakhshi is dying.'

The servants raced down the back alley and we swarmed up to the roof. When we ran down the steps to her house, we found Mattan Apa breathlessly calling on Allah.

'She hasn't been eating properly for months and after Nadira left, she's hardly talked to anyone either.'

Ammi lost her temper. 'Go and fetch Hazrat, you foolish woman, or you'll lose her. No, don't send anyone else. You'll have to go yourself because it was you who threw him out.' Mattan Apa lumbered down the stairs with unaccustomed speed.

We crowded into Bakhshi's room. Half her size, she lay, unconscious, face buried in a pile of pillows. I put my hand on her arm; her skin was burning. They were putting handkerchiefs soaked in perfumed water on her brow. I sent for ice and opened the windows. 'And Baji's not here,' Azizan whispered, tears running down her cheeks. Yes, Nadira should have been here.

But here was Hazrat, not looking too well himself. Apa got us all out, and left him with her. We stood in the gallery, some talking, some quiet. In a little while he looked out and asked for buttermilk. Apa almost fainted with relief as she relayed the request to Dulari below. He stayed in Bakhshi's room that night, and when we went over early next morning she was sitting up, looking pale and thin, but her usual calm self.

Miyan Jur'at, who had dozed outside their door all night, met us, smiling, and asked us to send someone to escort him to the Jagtey Jot dargah, where the two used to meet secretly and where he now wanted to make an offering in thanks. I hastened to write to Nadira; I knew she too had made a vow at the dargah for Bakhshi. Now she had to fulfil it.

'It's perfect,' Chapla said, laughing, when she returned a few days later and paid Bakhshi a visit. 'He's coming and going as usual. Meeting and parting keep the flame alive. Maybe you and I should do that. Meet in a different city every few months. Run into each other at mehfils here and there—everyone will think it's accidental but it will be planned. Our own secret. Wouldn't that be exciting?' Then, seeing my downcast face, she kissed my nose. 'Don't worry, little sparrow. We'll find a way to stay on in Delhi, perhaps. Or maybe I'll work at court here. Don't worry; trust me, you have nothing to worry about.' She sounded protective, almost as she did when talking to Kishen.

Could she get a permanent position as court dancer? There were so many competing for those well-paid positions and I was not experienced at court intrigues but I could try.

Delhi was less than three months away, but it seemed like three decades.

The day before she left she came in, in a sort of panic. 'It's stopped working, look.' She held out her long, slightly crooked fingers. The ring-watch had indeed stopped. 'What does it mean? What shall we do?'

'I'll get it mended,' I said calmly, pushing away Sharu's warnings that crowded into my head, and brushing with my lips the pulse beating at her wrist. 'I'll take it to Ram Awadh-ji right now.'

'What if he wants to keep it overnight? He usually does.'

'Then I'll send it to you through the next person who goes to Kashi. Someone or other is always going.'

'No, no, I want your ring. Bring it back if he can't do it today, and I'll get it fixed in Kashi.' I had never seen her so distraught.

It was high noon when I made my way to Ram Awadh's and after dark when I returned, because I had to sit at his shop and insist that it be mended right away. I knew that despite his promises to send it after me, he would find an excuse to delay it till a day or two later. 'Never trust any profession whose name ends with "i",' Ammi used to say sagely. Ridiculous, I thought, more likely never trust anyone at all to give you anything on time. Time—what would the Chinese man say to a watch stopping? Did it mean that the moment would last forever? Or that time had indeed run out? That Swiss watches aren't as good as they are reputed to be? Or that I had bought a fake?

'Wherever have you been?' Azizan was at the door when I returned. 'How could you spend the whole day out when they're leaving tomorrow?'

I mumbled something, and made my way upstairs, then over the rooftop and down to her room. She was kneeling on the floor, folding a few last pieces of clothing by the light of a candle. I took her hand and put the ring, warm from the pocket in my bodice, on to her finger. 'The door isn't locked,' she warned in a whisper against my throat as I slid her back on the carpet.

The next day, they set out at dawn, the sky already white as coals in a fire-bed. We embraced briefly in the midst of the melee and she turned to look back only once before the curtains fell over the bullock carts.

I turned, came up the stairs, and went straight to Munshi-ji to sort out some hitches in the month's budget. Then I lay on the floor of my room, unable to cry, unwilling to move. The room was unreal—everything, from walls to ceiling to the lizard crawling on it, was unreal.

The papiha called most of the night. Again and again. There was a full moon but I didn't wish to see either of them. I kept the curtains drawn.

For most of the next two months, I lay on the floor, staring at nothing. Or that's how I remember it. I couldn't have done just that. I met various people, and tried to get her a position at court, which proved harder than I had expected.

The first letter came, full of yearning. 'Why don't you come to me? Do you want to leave me alone here, with all these men and women pressing for my attention?' More came, and then more. I pictured her filled with longing for me. Absorbed in that image, I didn't think about what a letter is—a purveyor of moods that have passed by the time it reaches its destination. I drank in words like the dried-up earth drinking rain, and buried my face in clothes of mine she had worn and I hadn't washed, imbibing her scent.

On one of my brief forays out of my room, I heard another letter. As I passed Mahtab Baji's room, the girls were giggling, and Chand called out to me. 'Come listen to Miyan Rangin's letter from Banaras. He's written it to Baji.' Anything from Banaras I wanted to hear. Chand was reading aloud, with much comic gesticulation. It was addressed to Farkhanda, whom he described as 'a bouquet from the garden of intimacy and pleasure.' Then he went on to describe Banaras at length:

Ganga Jamuna baaham hain donon
Ek jism aur ek dam hain donon
Bahtey hain baaham jo dariya
Tirth hai yeh bara Hinduon ka
Ganga and Jamuna, both are one here
Both have one body and one breath
The two rivers flow conjoined
This is a very holy place for Hindus.

He went on to describe what various groups and individuals did on the banks of the river—Gujaratis, Khatris, Banias, Bengalis, some worshipping the sun, some bathing, some saying Shri Ram, some saying Bam Mahadev, some giving hidden charity, some setting flowers afloat. One prostrates himself, another sits in *asana*. One woman dries her hair, one plaits another's hair:

Ko'i apni saheliyon ko le saath
Dekar chalti hai haath mein haath
One takes her girlfriends with her,
They walk together hand in hand.

A lively description but it went on too long, and the rhyming was pedestrian. I was about to get up and leave, when the concluding peroration caught me though the verse hadn't improved:

Par chain mujhe kahin nahin hai
Main aap kahin hoon dil kahin hai
Teri hi qasam hai mujh ko har aan
Din raat rahe hai yahan tera dhyan . . .
Kya jaaniye dil tera ab kidhar hai
Hai aur taraf ko ya idhar hai
Par mujh ko yaqin hai a'e parizaad
Karti hogi tu raat din yaad
But I find no peace anywhere
I'm in one place and my heart in another
I swear by you, every moment,
I think of you here, day and night
Who knows where your heart is now—
Directed here or somewhere else?
But I'm sure, O fairy-born one,
You think of me, night and day.

The others started laughing. That Mahtab Baji should think of him, or indeed of anyone, night and day, seemed unlikely—I smiled a little and so did she.

Yah tujh ko samajh ke dil diya hai
Tu yaar hai aur bawafa hai
I've thought about it and given you my heart
You're my lover and you're faithful

Unimpressive though the verse was, it choked me up so I muttered something about feeling sleepy and left. Once, when everyone was away, performing in the ladies' quarters at the palace, I called her name repeatedly. It seemed inaudible. Years passed, and the heat blazed on, immoveable, in a near-absolute silence through which I gazed at little lines on paper. Uneasy drowsing, and one moment of painless waking before the ache began along the length of my body, as if half of it had been cut away. I should have been waiting but there seemed nothing to wait for. She had gone from me to others, into worlds I would never know.

No one else seemed to miss her particularly. If they missed anyone it was Nadira. Sharad had gone with Ratan to Hyderabad, so there was no one to notice me.

'Come, come to me. I can't bear it any longer.' This letter finally roused me to go and sit with the others, to ask around and find out that a cousin of Bakhshi's would be going to Kashi soon. I ran up to the blazing rooftop barefoot and arrived looking like a madwoman, my feet scorched. Bakhshi was practising but stopped when she saw me.

'Are you all right? Come in here.' She took me to her room and listened. 'Don't worry. I'm sure you can go with my cousin if Khala will let you.' Ammi quietly agreed, so

Dadda and I started packing. Suddenly, I felt light as air, ready to soar. All was well, as she had said it would be. I'd see the sacred city and we'd travel together to Delhi.

Two days before we were to leave, Heera came in with a letter while I was sitting with Munshi-ji. I forced myself to lay it aside and finish what I was doing. Then I ran to my room.

'Better not to come right now. There are a whole lot of visitors here, everyone is practising feverishly for Delhi, and we wouldn't have any time together. I don't want to upset Champa just yet. It's a matter of only a few weeks before we meet.'

Not quite sure what to think, and used to always giving in to her wishes, I started unpacking and re-read the letter, then decided not to; yes, it was just a matter of a few weeks before I'd have to pack for Delhi. Her usual practical approach to things, probably. Very much like my own streak of practicality. Or was there some reason she didn't state? Why did I obey what may have been just another mood? If I'd appeared at her door, what would she have done? Dadda and Ammi looked as if they wanted to ask questions but had decided to refrain.

I kept making plans for the future except that since they were all in my head, they seemed not quite real. To give them shape, I visited our Ustani and talked about possibly moving to Delhi or to Kashi. She gave me a dubious look. 'Why would you do that?'

'To live with Chapla,' I said defiantly, perhaps the only time I said this aloud.

'You're dreaming again,' was her response.

And then the letters stopped. The silence within became a silence without. I continued to write two, three letters almost every day, but in that last month the letter-carrier returned empty-handed.

Ammi noticed. 'What happened? Chapla stopped writing?'

'Well, we're meeting in Delhi very soon, so she probably thinks there's no need to write so often.'

'No need, no need.' For once, Mitthu sounded pensive.

6

Unfamiliar-looking buildings, much larger than ours but somehow grimmer, like the city itself, without the lime-washed sheen, the eager new whiteness. The emperor had been reinstated and the traitor tortured to death so order was restored and everyone's mood had lifted.

The morning they were to arrive, I found excuses to keep going out to the huge courtyard.

Here was the cavalcade. I stood just inside the gates, straining my eyes to see her. Here she was, and now all would be well. She came in, smiling, greeting everyone, but seemed not quite there—exhausted from the long journey, I told myself.

After the niceties and enquiries, the washing and feeding, I finally shut the door to our stuffy little room. She stood still, yielded to my embrace, then turned her face just enough for my lips to land on her cheek. A movement too slight to be measured.

My arms fell away. She began unpacking. Someone came to the door and called us. We went out. We ate, we talked. A wall heavy as that of a fortress between us, silence dense amid the chatter. The pleasant face which revealed nothing, which she showed everyone else, she now showed me too. Cold and warm like a stone in the sun.

Her mother hadn't come nor had Kishen. We'd been given one room, we were treated as a pair now, we were free in this city new to us. New as the door of the slaughter house at which one stands, stunned, unable to think, feel, move. We lay in one narrow bed, she turned on her side, her back to me, and seemed to sleep easily. Night after night, soundless tears, easy-flowing as blood.

We were staying in Chawri Bazaar, much larger and more crowded than our neighbourhood at home. Music filled the air in the evening as in our lane, drifting from every upper storey. The lanes were longer, more crowded than ours. In the day, merchants carried on their trade so the alleys were always crowded.

The house was full of dancers and musicians who had come to perform at the wedding so we were scarcely ever alone. I found myself asking trite questions that she answered smoothly or evaded with a joke. How was Champa? She was well. How were her other friends? They were well. The news, which I tried to think of as good, was that she had obtained a temporary position at the Kashi court.

Next afternoon, after rehearsing, a group of us escaped the frenzied preparations and went out towards the masjid that reflects the world, then through Urdu Bazaar to Johri Bazaar, the jewellers' market. I've been to Delhi many times since, so I know the road is splendid, wide enough for several elephants to walk side by side, a tree-shaded marble canal running down its centre, the buildings lining it all of the same height, with arched doors and windows and painted verandahs. But of that first walk I remember little except semi-dusk by day, the kind of uncertain light that dreams inhabit.

Crowds swam around me. I seemed to see buildings on fire, bellowing black smoke, bodies piling up, screams tearing the air, and blood, blood, everywhere. Just fifty years ago. And still earlier, more selective beheadings. At one end of our walk was the dargah of Sarmad the Sufi, and at the other end the small new gurudwara of the Sikh Guru Tegh Bahadur, both beheaded by the same emperor fifteen years apart.

Death at one blow or from bleeding drop after drop. Most fall somewhere in between.

Here was the square, built by a princess, Begam Sahib, her father's favourite. It was called by the name Mir Insha had given me, Chandni, because its central pool was made to reflect moonlight. Around it were shops arranged in a the shape of a crescent moon. The jewellery shops in Dariba Kalan and Dariba Khuld, the large and small streets of the incomparable pearl, were open once more but the Delhi girls said they were nothing to what they had been before the Persian brigand looted them and killed thousands. I had planned to buy us matching sets of enamelled bracelets with paired fish or peacocks, but the idea of being a pair now seemed childish. Nor could I look at anything except her as she drifted ahead of me, pausing to consider small items on stalls. My pearl unparalleled, mine no longer. More likely, never mine.

Winter rain in Delhi. Skies closing down above, river ominous, grey. No romance to these cold showers and muddy puddles through which riders and drivers forged, indifferent to those they splashed.

I looked at her but saw nothing. I spoke to her, as if speaking to someone who never raised her veil, the way shopkeepers in the market speak to many women customers. I didn't ask the real questions, dreading the answers; she talked in riddles. Not finding the right words, I fell silent, and my movements became even clumsier than usual. I picked up a goblet of unfamiliar proportions, and it tilted, drenching our host's carpet. She efficiently mopped it up while I watched. From being necessary to being a pleasant superfluity is a journey one can take in a few weeks, maybe less.

She danced at the wedding, her luminescence undimmed, spreading, scintillating. Outside the circle now, I watched as people flocked around her, seeking acquaintance. Noor, the bride, seemed already thousands of miles away, her face pale despite being plastered with colour, belying her name. One world slams its doors and another drags you in its wake against your will.

The night before she was to leave, we returned to some semblance of our former selves but only the way a shadow resembles the figure that casts it. While the others went on yet another shopping spree, we slipped away and walked further, to the larger garden built by Begam Sahib's murderous sister Roshanara. We kissed briefly in the shadow of the doomed princess's tomb.

So different from the gardens of my city—this dark place with its tall palms, its light shadowed even at noon. The city of gardens edged by desert; thorny plants should have grown here instead of leafy ones.

Next morning, she sprang early from bed where we had slept once more cheek to cheek. 'I meant to talk,' she said ruefully, as if the time for that had passed, and perhaps it had. We went out amid dawn chants and bells, and sat on the steps of the mosque, watching cleaners, scavengers, cows, crows, pigeons, workers hurrying to their destinations.

'Centre of the world,' she said.

'As Isfahan once was.'

'Or Athens.'

'Or Pataliputra.'

'Or London,' she ended sombrely. And then, nestling on my shoulder, 'Take me home to your city.'

She left, this time with many backward looks; dazed, I returned to our room, and found a note on the pillow. 'We are too far apart. Even pigeons find it hard to fly that far. Let me go, little sparrow.'

I sat down, then lay down, pierced by more bullets than were needed to fell me.

The busy programme my mother had planned for the month kept me moving through the days and concealed me from observation. But from the night there was no escape. The repetitive circling of events like a wheeling hawk, trying and trying to discover what went wrong and when and how and why. Raised on the poets' laments, hadn't I always known that everything must and will go wrong some time? Did it help that there was a verse for each twist of the knife?

One day, I walked alone to the river, swollen by the rains, ferocious and grey under a lowering sky. The river of passion, of separation, Mir Insha had called it. Passion had not proved strong enough to swallow us after all; it had thrown us up, flotsam on banks far apart. Too far to swim, too far to fly.

And so, home. Her first letter came. Endearments, adjurations, descriptions, apologies, self-recriminations that I hastily countered in my letters, and grief—grief that I couldn't quite comprehend, for hadn't she made the decision? When you're drowning, fighting for each breath, you can't inhabit the pain of one who holds on to the crumbling riverbank. Her letters consoled, telling me she would always be attached to me, but I longed for the impossible - a complete explanation. Those she gave didn't satisfy my hunger. Why tastes change, why hearts wander—as well try to explain the stars as they streak across the sky.

I still sent her poems and she sent a couple, then she stopped. Perhaps she had stopped writing? Or was writing for others' eyes.

Thought, and fear, fear that had lurked but not emerged into the open, besieged me now at every turn of the mind, now that I had to focus not on her but myself.

One long and solitary afternoon, I drank first one, then another glass of wine. An old remedy. Soon the goblet was empty and I was lapped in dreamless sleep. This became my afternoon routine. I'd wake up, heavy-headed, and rush to the mehfil. More glasses afterwards, to take me through to the early hours of morning. I was in charge of supplies and accounts; if the servants noticed, they may have thought my guests were drinking more than usual or they may have chosen not to comment.

One afternoon, I returned from my usual meeting with Munshi-ji, and as I entered my room and headed straight for the wine, two figures sitting in the silent semi-darkness turned.

'Who? Nadira? Sharad? When did you arrive?'

'Just now. Didn't want to make an ado and have to answer questions right away so came here first.'

Death was in the room, on Sharad's face, in Nadira's eyes.

'Rangin Sahib told us about Ratan.' He had, indeed, but, shameful to say, I found it so hard just to get through the days and nights that this death of someone I barely knew hadn't affected me as it should have. 'How did it happen?' I sat down next to Sharad.

'I don't know. It was like lightning striking. He had a fever at night, not too high, and before morning he was gone. With no warning. Just like that.'

'Were you there?'

'Not at that moment. I grew tired, he seemed to be asleep, and I fell asleep in the next room. His mother was with him but she didn't hear anything. No one could believe it.'

'And . . .?' I looked at Nadira.

'He brought me back with him,' she said.

'His first wife was making her life hell. She wouldn't say so but I could see it. She was half-starved, holed up in a room, in parda, with one untrained little maid, and no one to talk to her or take her out. Thanks to the maids, we managed to exchange notes.'

'And what did Akbar Ali Sahib say?'

'He's a coward, couldn't stand up to his wife. I told her she had to leave and not renew the *muta'a*.'

Nadira threw off her shawl as if overheated and I saw what I'd missed. She caught my eye and smiled ruefully. 'Pray it's a girl. Because I'm not having any more after this one.'

It was a girl, named for Azizan. A month before the birth, fever flowed through the city, carrying away many, John Mordaunt Sahib among them. Azizan was sick for just two days. Others were sick too, in our houses, but she was the only one to succumb. I didn't catch it. Perhaps I was immune, in this narrower, safer, windowless world. Nadira's last link with her mother was gone, but she had me, and then the baby.

To protect the baby from the fever, Nadira moved her into my room and we took turns waking at night to attend to her. This was an unusual arrangement but after her experience with Bakhshi, Mattan Apa had become more lenient. Ammi probably realized that I needed this as much as Nadira, even if I didn't know it.

An unlikely apparition in my room—baby Azzo, fat little arms curved above her head in sleep, perfect lashes curled on her cheek. One afternoon, tired, I put her to sleep and she settled on my chest, one fist firmly closed on my finger. A new weight on my heart, this, after the first one had slipped away. I couldn't move so I had to fall asleep too. Dadda and Heera took care of her when Nadira and I were working. Most mothers among us travel often, and children are raised by the whole household.

At first, Nadira slept on the rug but gradually she moved into my bed. It happened over the next two years, almost without my noticing it. That finally put an end to my night-time weeping but I couldn't give up wine. I had to gulp it down in the storeroom, and chew cardamom afterwards. Nadira either didn't notice or more likely was too worn out to remonstrate with me.

After a while I secreted in my dressing room a small French wine glass that Madan had given me. I could always refill it in the afternoon when everyone was asleep.

There was another newcomer besides the baby—an eight-year-old orphan called Sundar whom Ammi brought with her from Delhi. 'She likes babies,' Ammi said vaguely. 'She can help you look after Azzo.' Nadira and I exchanged glances; this waif with her peaked face and skinny limbs seemed herself to need looking after.

Ammi was right. Sundar cheered up at the sight of the baby, and took to carrying her around, bathing and feeding her, like a child with a doll.

At every parting, a self dies. When all the selves go, does one reach the real one or turn to nothing? With Azizan, one of my selves died—the child who had once resented Nadira's new foster-sister, that pale girl who, not content with Shirin's company, insisted on turning our twosome into a threesome. That constantly questioning, slightly annoying presence who was perhaps a version of me. Bakhshi, though Nadira's friend, was remote in some way hard to define, but Azizan lived in the same house with Nadira who had been mine first.

Is it you, then, I miss, who now live elsewhere, or is it the girl of the unbaked pitcher who sank down, down, into the grey river in the grey city, and never returned to her own?

~

'Nawab Sahib couldn't stop weeping at Mordaunt's funeral,' Sharad told me. 'He cried like a small child.' And he never recovered, never became his old cheerful self again, the one who was always searching out new sights, objects, sensations.

'I'm moving back to the village,' Sharad announced a few months later. 'This city is tiring me out. Come and see me there.'

I went, some weeks after he moved. The house was simple, compared to the mansions he had worked on. Limewashed walls, and on one of them a vast, many-coloured Durga, her tiger almost smiling.

Having gone to bed early because everyone did and there was nothing to do after dark, I woke early and walked barefoot into the orchard. In the distance, caught in a golden web, deer grazed and peacocks shrieked.

Sharad followed me. 'Do you want a baby deer to take back with you? Yours died, right?'

'No, not just yet. One baby is enough. Maybe when she's a little older and can play with it.'

We turned back to the house. The rain had stopped and the wet grass was carpeted with white stars, orange-touched, rice grains half-dyed in saffron. Their scent encircled us like heavenly light. Which reminds me, as I write, of Noor, that pale young bride from Delhi. If only

De Boigne had left her here instead of changing her name to Helene, taking her to his land and then leaving her for a younger woman. How can she bear to live so far from flowers she grew up with?

I picked one up to smell and it brushed my lips.

'Shefali,' said Sharad. 'My mother's favourite.'

'I thought it was called Harsingar?'

'Yes, because it's Shiv-ji's adornment, and it's the only flower that can be picked up from the ground and still offered.'

When she touches something silky, does she remember the skin she called silken? Or has another touch overlaid it?

Dadda, who was sitting on the verandah, said, 'It has many names. Paarijaat too—do you know the story of that name?'

'No.'

'There was a beautiful princess called Paarijaataka who was enamoured of the sun. The sun returned her feelings and they had a short, hot romance. But the sun has many things to do, he has to shine on all the world. He left her and she despaired and killed herself. The tree grew from her ashes and that's why the flowers fall to the ground when the sun's first ray touches them. They fall like tears because the tree can't bear to look at the sun.'

'Maybe I can plant it in our courtyard?'

'They say it won't flourish if you plant it yourself. Someone else has to secretly plant it for you.'

~

Two in one, dogaana, we call it. Fused centres, with skin, flammable skin, holding together interiors, flesh, juice, fibers.

Next summer, walking again in Sharad's orchard in the brief cool at dawn, I picked up a doubled mango that had fallen under a tree. Plump, heart-shaped. The papiha called insistently, preparing to leave its babies in others' nests. I looked around—in this clearing, a group of us had once put up a swing. Here, she had climbed, lithe as a monkey, to fasten the strings to a bough, and then stood behind me on the seat, ankles pressing into my sides.

The mango lay heavy in my hand, its green skin smooth and dry.

One of the gardeners went by and on an impulse, I asked what made fruit grow doubled like this one.

'I'm not sure why it happens, bibi,' he said. 'But I think it happens more when the trees are stressed. In years when there's less rain. Last year it was a good rainy season but this year not a cloud in sight.' He walked on, shaking his head.

I walked in the opposite direction, and was assailed by a chorus of shrieks. A flock of *saatbhai*, seven brothers; the English call them seven sisters. One had another pinned down and was mercilessly tearing at it. It lay still, as if dead. I shooed the aggressor away. The assaulted one sat up, shook itself, and flew off, while the rest chattered at a distance.

Delhi. Its old stones dark with blood, layer beneath layer of pain lying who knows how deep under streets and buildings. How could we have imagined our bond would flourish there the way it did in this young city that had never known mass slaughter? In those harsh skies the thread was bound to get cut, leaving the spool forlorn and the kite floundering.

We still exchanged letters, though less frequently. The same pet names for a while, the same assurances that now had a somewhat different meaning, accounts of our lives with crucial facts omitted, and new offerings. 'If you ever need anything, let me know and I'll be there,' she wrote. A promise she kept. Teaching and looking after Azzo as if she were her own daughter.

For a few months, I puzzled over details with Sharad, and for several more years by myself, scanning each word in old letters for a clue. Was it my inexperience, my importunities? Does too much of a thing produce its opposite? Were we too alike? Or too different? Was our closeness just the clutching of desire, fear, loneliness? Had I driven her away by talking too much? Or not enough? Had I waited too long, so that we had too little time together? All the theories seemed equally plausible and equally unconvincing.

'I wish I could go somewhere else, not live in that house or that city,' I said savagely.

'It wouldn't make any difference. You'd carry it with you.' Sharad was gazing out of the window but not looking at anything, desultorily puffing at the hookah. His locks were silvering and still abundant, but the hair on the top of his head was thinning.

'We seemed so perfect together. There were no problems at all.'

'Maybe she didn't think so. And if nothing else, the distance was a problem. You're eating too many sweets.' I kept picking them up as we talked and the plate was almost empty. 'And drinking too much wine.' In his house,

I didn't need to hide my drinking. 'Do you know you've put on quite a lot of weight?' With those close to him, he was outspoken, even abrupt.

I covered up my embarrassment by brazening it out. 'Who cares—what difference does it make? No one comes to the kotha to gaze at me.' In poems, they all become skeletons like Majnun, but in life emptiness takes different shapes. 'When are you coming to town next?'

'When I have business there, I suppose. Probably next month.'

'Don't you miss your friends?'

'Many of them come here. Insha Sahib and Jur'at Miyan were here last week. Insha Sahib was asking about you. He said you seem to be hiding.'

'How is he? I heard the literary quarrels with Mushafi Sahib have started up again?'

'Yes, he can't forgive Insha Sahib for doing him so many favours, introducing him into Mirza Shukoh's court, for example. And both of them are equally pugnacious.'

'Mushafi Sahib is older. Shouldn't he have more sense?'

'When did the old ever have more sense? Also, he has a bunch of crazy students who incite him. They are far from literary—they go out on the streets like a pack of wild dogs, yelping against his rivals. One of them has taken the pen-name Gharam.'

Despite myself, I started laughing. 'Hot in person or in verse?'

'Neither, if you ask me, though I'm sure he thinks he's hot on the market. He and another one both work in Mirza Shukoh's ammunition house. Maybe that's where he got the idea for his name. I hope the weapons he makes are sharper than his poems. Oh, speaking of poets, I nearly forgot—Miyan Jur'at said to give this to you and Nadira. He said he'll come to see you one of these days.' He took a paper from his writing desk.

> <u>A Chronogram for the Death of Azizan Tawaif</u>
> On a fresh, blooming flower, a splendid city,
> Alas that autumn's wind should blow.
> A rose garden's pride in springtime—alas,
> That a bud should feel the hand of death.
> Here where red wounds burn liver and heart—
> What can the breast be but a furnace?
> Alas! Alas! Curses on fate that killed one
> Whose ways enraptured one and all.
> Why shouldn't sorrow's mountain fall on mourners' hearts
> When that flower-like body lies in the dust?
> A rare pearl has left the world's ocean of verse—
> Why shouldn't tears flow from the eyes like dew?
> Weeping, Jur'at said this date of departure, alas!
> One dear as life [*aziz-e jaan*] went thus into the dust.

'How's Nadira taking it?'

'Little Azzo keeps her so busy I think she doesn't have much time to dwell on it. Whenever she's not working she's sleeping.'

'Lucky her. Finding it hard to sleep these days. And when I do, I have such mixed-up dreams.'

'I slept well last night, here. In my room, it's difficult. I've moved things around, but still . . .'

'Try some warm milk with turmeric last thing at night.'

I laughed. 'You sound like Chapla. But I don't like milk—except to write notes with. Poor Dadda, she was really disappointed when I told her I'd gone off milk again.'

He chuckled. 'She'll be even more disappointed if you tell her you've taken to wine instead. I'm surprised she hasn't noticed. Why don't you move to another room? That might help.'

'Maybe.'

When I got back, I managed to exchange rooms with Chand; that was as far as I could move. The window of my old room looked out on the lane, and the interior gallery looked over the yard, the back alley and the city. In the new room, the window was kept closed because it was in the shared wall with the next house. From the gallery, I saw just our yard and the kitchen, unless I craned my neck. But that was enough. I had no desire to see more. As Insha Sahib says,

Apni aankhon mein us pari ke baghair
Shahar aabaad aur ujaar hai ek

In my eyes, without that fairy,
It's all one, the city teeming or empty.

Was the kiss in Roshanara Bagh our last? But there were others later, when I was asleep. Is a dream as real as the past? I remembered her saying, 'Only if two people have the same dream.'

7

A fugitive girl looking for somewhere to put down her things, somewhere to sleep. She hides in a room where several others live, stows her bags under one bed, and lies motionless under another. She's afraid to move but a spreading pool betrays her. They drag her out, berate her, say she must pay them. She has no money so they say they will sell her things and they start going through her bags. They lift out my books, and she says, 'Don't sell those, they were my grandmother's.'

Sharad walked in and opened the curtains on light and sound. 'What are you doing? Brooding as usual?'

I rubbed my eyes. 'No, half asleep. When did you get here?'

'Yesterday. Mir Insha summoned me.'

'And you thought it would be a good idea to wake me at the crack of dawn? Oh, wait, it's later than I thought.'

'Yes. You're making up for lost sleep. Where's the baby?'

'Nadira took her over to see Mattan Apa. They generally spend the morning there.'

As usual, he was examining everything in the room. 'Where did this picture come from? It's new, isn't it?'

'Chapla sent it a few days ago. For my birthday.'

'Oh no, I forgot your birthday again.'

'That's all right. I don't expect boys to remember such things. I might not remember myself if Dadda wasn't so ready with her knotted string.'

'Interesting.' He was absorbed in the painting; he has a way of getting completely into something for a moment, then freeing himself and moving on as if he never had the least interest in the matter. 'Two girls on a rooftop that looks like it could be anyone's house, not the usual palace. No lotuses or peacocks. And that golden ring round the golden moon is a nice touch. Also, the way they're looking at each other. Those stark reds and yellows in the moonlight, though—they should have been lighter colours.' He put it down. 'But listen, I came to ask you something. Mir Insha is writing a book on language and he wants everyone to help by collecting words, and he asked me to ask you. He thinks you the most intelligent one here. What do you say?'

'What language? Farsi?'

'No. Well, the book is in Farsi but it's about our language— Hindi, the language of Hind. Urdu some call it now. It's a first—the first grammar book.'

'Who needs a grammar book? We know the grammar.'

'But lots of others don't. Many newcomers, from Bihar, Punjab, Bengal, and the Afghans, the Pathans, the Baghdadis, the Turks, the Iranis, the English, the French, the Swiss . . .'

'All right, all right, stop.' I pretended to cover my ears. 'I'll help. What sort of help?'

'He says language changes, and he wants to trace the changes. One question is, which words, which phrases to include and which to exclude. He wants to include many newer words.'

This was something I had wondered about off and on. Persian, Arabic, Awadhi—were all those words equally good? What about Punjabi or English? Insha Sahib had used English words in his poems—*botal*, lady, powder.

'What kind of phrases?' I asked. 'Common ones or unusual ones?'

'Both. Everything you hear anyone use—nursemaids and midwives, porters, wandering traders, vendors, new girls. So many people pass through your house.'

'Yes, and speak languages from so many different regions.'

'Exactly. He says that any word women start using becomes part of the language.'

'All women?'

'Here's Rangin Sahib, he'll explain.' That gentleman had just put his head round the curtain. No doubt he'd come straight from Mahtab Baji's room.

'*Arey*, how come everyone has decided to congregate here in the morning today?' I sprang out of bed and wrapped myself in the large shawl Sharad had taken off.

'Just the two of us came, to talk to you.'

'I'll be back in a minute.' When I returned, having washed up, they were drinking sugarcane juice and still discussing the matter.

'Women!' pronounced Rangin Sahib, turning to me. 'Words that women use become the language. Who teaches us to speak as children? Women do—mothers, nurses. Begams and Bais both.'

'Don't you mean the women of Delhi, though?' asked Sharad.

'Yes, but Gul Bai came from there, so though these girls grew up here, they speak the language of Shahjahanabad. Much better than those newcomers from the provinces who live in Delhi these days and think they are Dilliwalas.'

'That's what Mir Insha says,' I put in. 'I'm not so sure.'

'It's true. You know, I learnt the language for my *rekhti* from all of you, actually first from the *khangis* in Delhi. But afterwards from women here too. I made a glossary of the words and phrases women use, and Insha Sahib is going to include it in his book, mentioning my name.' He looked pleased with himself.

The khangis—those married women who smuggled themselves into—well, not into our kotha, Ammi didn't need them nor did she want the trouble, but into some lower-status kothas—to meet clients, while their husbands looked the other way. Sometimes I despised them for their duplicitous ways and other times I felt sorry for them. It can't be easy to pretend all the time and follow different rules in different places.

'What's the book to be called?' I asked after a few minutes.

'*Darya-e Latafat.*'

'Good name—the only real pleasure is in words perhaps.'

'Real, I don't know. Longer lasting—yes. Always changing, yet the same, like an ocean or a river.'

Into that river I plunged and surfaced refreshed. I retrieved one of Munshi-ji's old desks, brought it to my room, and tried recording words, phrases, conversations. Had this happened two years earlier, Ammi might have thought I was wasting my time but now she knew I needed to occupy my mind with more than my usual work.

Our friends were interested and contributed titbits. Sharu giggled at the list of words for men who dress and behave like women.

'There are more,' he said. 'There's *amir khaani*, and then for a whole group together there's *kouwa guhaar*.'

'Should we include such strange words?'

'Strange, strange,' interjected Mitthu, savouring the sound.

'Let's put everything in, and then he can remove what he likes.'

'True, he's got phrases like *bazaar ki mithai* for a woman of the marketplace. That's not much better.'

'Oh, sweets - that reminds me,' cried Sharu. 'There's *dandaan misri* for a delicate man.'

'That's the sweet we make for small children,' I said. 'Kishen was crazy about it. And Sundar still is, though she pretends to be all grown up.' I smiled at her; she had brought baby Azzo in and was singing softly to her in a corner.

'Yes, it melts in the mouth. *Khaasi pyaari*.' Sharu was still reading from the list. 'But you girls also call each other that, right?'

'Yes, and *vaari* too. That's on both lists.'

Oblivious, he continued, 'Look, here's a whole mix of words from all over the place, even *chapla*, which means *bijli*. Shouldn't he separate them out into words from Farsi, words from Sanskrit, and so on?'

'Maybe he wants to show how mixed it all is, like cement, as *rekhta* is?' I kept my head bent, as I wrote the new words.

"If only Ratan were here," Sharu replied. "He had such a mixed bunch of friends – from noblemen, noblewomen and khwajasarai to laborers, bankas, hijras and vendors. He knew them all by name, remembered everything about each one, and they all adored him."

That evening, Insha Sahib himself came over.

'I'm so tired,' he moaned. 'I've been roaming the city all week, going to gathering after gathering, and seeing the same faces in each. Where's that boy?'

'He's gone downstairs to stretch his legs. I have a question. Do you want to include words from Bangla? People go to Kalkatta and come back with words.'

'Why not? Put down any words you hear people using. Bengalis are hilarious. If they see five male elephants, they'll refer to them as female and if they see five female ones, they'll refer to them as male.'

'That's because in Bangla words are neither male nor female.'

'I know, but you'd think they'd occasionally get it right, just by chance. But no, they always manage to reverse it.' I couldn't help laughing at this exaggeration.

'Where else are you going to collect words?'

'All sorts of places. I've been talking to the daily wage labourers in the marketplace. Some really funny conversations I've had with them. Oh yes, I'm making a list of vendors' cries too—write down any that you think of. I'm going to Kashi tomorrow, by the way. Anything you want to send?'

'Yes, I'll send something small if it's not too much trouble.' I kept my eyes averted.

His eyes on me forced me to look up. His voice changed from its usual bantering tone, slowed down. 'You had the real thing, you know—the gem not to be found by searching. I saw your face when you were together. You are very fortunate—don't forget that. Be grateful.'

Sharad returned just then and he turned to him with a joke.

~

Tomorrow is my mother's birthday, I want to buy her some fabric as a surprise so I plan to go to Motilal-ji's shop instead of calling him over. In the late afternoon I look out of my window. It faces east and there are no houses to block the view. A black, crinkly line appears on the horizon, in an instant more such lines run upward and cover the sky; it turns black and rain starts. Five minutes, and it clears, the sky turns blue again. I alight from the palanquin between two shops facing each other. Both are about to close but I start looking through the wares. Pale blue, pale green, pale pink. For Azizan, for Chapla, for my mother? Fabrics spread over my lap, trailing on the floor, I feel the after-rain cold run through me, and I think, Is my mother alive? Is it her birthday? What month is this?

~

One afternoon, after a long and somewhat tipsy nap, I stepped out out into the gallery. Down in the courtyard, the maids were sorting spices, and on the roof the girls were painting their toe-nails or oiling their hair. The brief hour before preparation for the long evening. Ammi's life-work, clustered here, and in our hands now. We had gotten our baby deer after all, and Sundar had named her Saloni. She was feeding pieces of fruit to baby girl and baby deer by turns. She held each piece above their heads, and Saloni stood on her hind legs while Azzo crowed and held up her hands. She was at the age when babies turn plump as ripe melons. I saw Kishen chortling as Chapla threw him up in the air and caught him, glee reflected from one face to the other. How did he look now, and she?

Nadira came down from the roof to the gallery, oddly flustered and thoughtful at the same time. 'Let's go up,' she said. 'You go ahead, I'm coming.'

While I was answering the girls' desultory questions about the book, she went into our room and then came up, wearing a new gold gauze dupatta, and holding a bowl of cardamoms. She plopped down and put one in my hand. 'Open it and count the seeds.'

I hesitated, knowing what was coming, then pinched it open, and carefully separated the seeds on my palm.

'Twelve.' All the girls had stopped what they were doing and were intently watching us.

She held out her hand. 'Mine has eleven.' So I was the 'male.' She put the seeds in my mouth, silky and warm from her hand, and I could feel my face heat up as I put my seeds between her lips.

The girls burst out laughing, cheering, and demanding a wedding feast. Nadira pulled her dupatta forward so that it covered both our heads. For a moment, our faces were close together in the sunlight slanting through the gauze. Then she slid it backward on to my head, pulled mine away and put it over her head. A poor exchange for her; mine was ordinary cotton.

Later that evening, I was taking a quick sip when Azzo toddled up and put out her hand for the glass in a practiced way. I hastily put it on a high shelf. Nadira walked in, went straight to the shelf, took down the glass, put it on an uncarpeted piece of floor and stamped on it with her high-heeled shoe.

'No more,' she said to me. 'Promise.' I promised. As Sharu had once said, she was my everyday food and drink, the space of home. I would have to do without wine.

8

Two years before I saw her again. Though I saw her many times on the street, and still see her occasionally, head bent, lost in thought, then some other woman turns around.

We continued to exchange letters, some filled with fond echoes though words had changed their meanings, others slightly bitter, others reticent, until they dwindled to nothing. She was busy, no doubt, and so was I—new ties and old ones turned new, the pleasure and exhaustion of tending the baby. She became an undersong, or a song heard from another house across the lane even as someone else is singing in one's own room.

Then she arrived to perform at prince Wazir Ali's wedding, the grandest the city had ever seen. By then, Mattan Apa was gone, and Ammi had retreated into a space of her own. Nadira and I found ourselves in charge and began to run the two establishments as one, more profitable, enterprise. We bought up the small kotha in between our houses, and did a good deal of reconstruction, connecting all three buildings. In the course of this work, I moved once more, this time into Shirin's old room, which was next door to my old room. Heera, who had moved after her marriage, could now manage the kitchen and stores for all of us once more, and Dadda didn't need to constantly shuffle between the two households. I had much more work, overseeing the finances; Munshi-ji had always kept accounts for both houses.

The walls had come down between the houses, and a wall had come up between Chapla and me; it had chinks through which we caught glimpses of one another but the treasure chambers had closed their doors—forever?

Rupa was with her; I never really knew the details of how they first met or when. Chapla told fragments of a story but her stories were patchwork, with rough parts neatly smoothed over. Rupa reminded me of myself in some ways—plain and quiet, a ferociously churning mind behind the withheld exterior. But they shared a city, a heritage—perhaps that is stronger glue than the language of poetry.

They stayed only a couple of days. Nadira and she were excessively polite to each other. She spent a lot of time playing with the children and with Saloni. Once she too had been fawn-like; she seemed less easily startled now. Azzo, babbling non-stop, followed Kishen, who was gangly and long-legged, like a chick following its mother. Rarely did her eyes smile at me. Windows with curtains half-drawn, who knew what was going on in the light inside that scarcely filtered through. Perhaps she dropped the veil with Rupa, when they walked together, arms entwined, heads leaning towards one another.

It was that year Mir Rangin forded his own dark river. His friend Miyan Qadir, who was now Chand's patron, told us about it. Mir Rangin turned forty that year and perhaps that set him off. Or perhaps he was worn out by his two wives and many children. As was to be expected, he was no longer as enthralled by Mahtab Baji either.

'You know he left town when the Nawab died five years ago,' I told Chapla as I reclined on the divan and she sat upright across the room, hugging her knees, miles away. The year after you left. 'Suddenly, he reappeared. He was raving about how the world is transient, how no one helps you when you most need it, and how wives and children are enemies who eat what they can and then leave you to die alone.' As I was speaking, I wondered once more why I became so voluble in her presence.

'Sounds like *Bhaja Govindam*—your family members talk to you only as long as you're earning.'

'He wouldn't eat and he wouldn't sleep and then he suddenly disappeared again. After a couple of months, he turned up at the house of his friend Miyan Qadir and his brother. Miyan Qadir told me that he was a wreck but they made him rest and eat, and he recovered. Then, one day, they were trying to organize his papers which were a mess, and they found his book about horses. It was in prose and they told him he must put it into verse for their sakes. And he did it—in just twenty days!'

'He has a gift for writing fast, as fast as his horses.'

'He knows everything about horses,' said Nadira, coming in with Sharad. Sundar had taken Rupa to the market to buy gifts for people in Kashi. 'He's fought in so many battles, and travelled everywhere—how many cities—twenty? Thirty?'

'Yes, easily that many. And he does know all about horses—the breeds, the diseases, the cures. It's a useful book.'

'Horses for Rangin Sahib and elephants for Insha Sahib,' put in Sharad. 'Did you know his latest poem is about a romance between his elephants?'

'Which ones? Chanchal Pyari?' I had seen her at his house; she had a slightly mischievous look and seemed always to be smiling, her mouth hanging slightly open.

'Yes. His elephant Bahadur, who was captured in Beri district, fell for Chanchal Pyari. After they first met, they were kept apart for a year and he pined and groaned for her. Finally, they united and the whole world rejoiced—at least in the poem it did.'

'And they lived happily together?'

'No, he says this is life, not a romance. He tells the story as it really happened. One day, Bahadur came to Chanchal and she was in a bad mood so she kicked him. He left and he didn't look back. He took up with another female, but he never found happiness again.'

'Happiness—is there such a thing?'

I laughed. 'Only in romances, like the Hindu princess of Kashmir's happiness when she marries the Muslim prince in Rangin Sahib's romance, remember, the one in which he said that those who dressed in white had lost the desire for pleasure?' As I spoke the words, heat washed over me—she in my bodice, stars sinking and rising, in white once more as when I first saw her, drawing me by the hand away from the crowd. My face burnt. She would think I was deliberately referring to our past.

But she answered soberly, as if she had noticed nothing, 'What I liked about that romance was the way he explained the princess's dislike for men—she was a bird in an earlier birth, remember, and her mate deserted her when a forest fire broke out?'

This allowed me to recover. 'Yes, and she remembers that birth. He doesn't explain how or why, or say that she imagined it.'

We batted the ball between us once again; about ideas we could still talk freely.

The next time she came, six years later, she and I went to Qadam-e Rasool which had just been built. Afterwards, we walked in the rocky garden around it, and talked about others, partly to avoid talking about ourselves.

'So your Shirin finally married her prince,' she said. 'Why didn't you come for the wedding? I thought you would.'

'I wasn't well. Some stomach thing. Ammi was worried about leaving me, but Dadda nursed me through it.'

'Really? Are you all right now?'

'Yes.'

'Are you sure? You look a bit pulled down. You must boil ginger in water and drink it with honey every day. And eat curds with bananas to keep up your strength.'

'All right.'

'Don't laugh. Will you do it?'

'I will.'

'I'll tell Dadda, and she'll prepare it for you. There's Sundar coming out now. What a pious girl she is. Bowing to every temple and dargah we passed on the way. And she's certainly grown up to match her name.'

'Yes, Azzo adores her.'

'I know. And I hear the Nawab likes her too?'

'Yes, too much, but the foolish girl is more interested in a storyteller from Pratapgarh. The Nawab heard about it, and told her he would keep paying her salary, but he wouldn't force her to keep him company—because there's no pleasure in it if it's undesired.'

'A true prince.'

'Hmm. But after his father died, he dismissed Mirza Hasan Raza, and the poor man died in great poverty a few months ago.'

'That's unkind. Did no one help him?'

'Mir Almas Ali Khan—who else? And the Resident Sahib too.'

'And what happened to Raja Tikait Rai?'

'He's living quietly with his family.'

'At least his buildings will keep his name alive—all the temples and tanks.'

'Yes, and the imambara, and the red stone ghat at Kanpur.'

'Is Bakhshi still with Hazrat?'

'Oh, yes. He still comes and goes. He puts her name along with his at the end of all his poems.'

'Really? They probably write them together.' Our poems—that we wrote together—do you remember them?

'How's Mir Insha?'

'He's moved from Mirza Shukoh's palace to the Nawab's.'

'So he's a royal poet now?'

'Yes, he was thrilled at first but now it exhausts him. He has to be as much an entertainer as a poet. Has to produce a new joke every day and laugh at all the Nawab's jokes. He's even collecting them in a book.'

'Are they good?'

'Sharu and the boys find them funny. I think many of them are silly. Like this one—he and Shafai Khan were sitting with the Nawab, and Shafai Khan said, "These jokes which drop from Huzoor's lips like the water of heaven will get lost if they're not written down", and then he put his hand in his undergarment pocket and took out an inkpot. The Nawab commented, "How do you manage such a big inkpot when you sit down and stand up?"'

She smiled. 'Boys never cease to be fascinated by their bodies. Making jokes about them may be better than taking them too seriously—bodies are funny, don't you think? What happened to his book on language?'

When we were younger, we would have added something about the absurdity of body parts that rise on their own like flags at the Residency and then eject like fountains, and would have dissolved into uncontrollable giggling; now, we just smiled.

'Delayed by all this other stuff he has to do. But it will get done, Sharad says. Rangin Sahib helped, and so did Sharu and I. We collected many kinds of words.'

'Yes, I heard. I wish I could have helped too. I miss our conversations, our reading and writing together.'

'So do I. What are you reading now?'

'I'm trying to read Natya Shastra, but it's difficult, and the more I read the more I realize how little I know. Once you said happiness exists only in romances. Maybe that's true. But *ananda* is different—it's in oneself and is awakened in different ways, mainly through conversation with someone of like heart.'

'Do you mean a teacher?'

'Yes, but maybe more than one. Like watching different types of dances and dramas, not just one.'

'Many, not one, lead to the one?'

'Something like that. How are your many ones? What is Sharu up to in his village?'

'Rearing cats and dogs and deer and ornamental ducks. Planning gardens and orchards and tanks. Collecting glassware from round the world. He still designs some buildings but now that he's in the village we don't see him as much.'

'His family got him back after all.'

'Yes.' Families do get back their own. Families of one kind or another. We had descended the slope. 'Would you like to go to the new Hanuman temple that Begam Rabia built? Sundar goes quite often, she can take us.'

'Yes, very much. I meant to ask you to take me.' She paused. 'Is there a bakul tree there? To the right of the door?'

'I don't know.'

She laid her arm lightly across my shoulders. 'Let's go and see.'

'Why?' I asked, trying to keep the tremor out of my voice.

'They say if you wish for a child at a temple with such a tree, you get it.'

The temple was small as all temples here are, different from the big ancient ones in the Dakkan that Sharu described. Quiet now because it was early afternoon. From the glaring sun into musky darkness. And at its centre, a lamp with a steady flame. No whisper of wind to shake it. A bell chiming gently. She sat down at the shrine and I stood in the doorway. Flame in my heart, unwavering; keep it in yours.

She turned back and touched my forehead with vermilion.

Next year, she had her son. Mohan, another version of Kishen. It was a difficult pregnancy, she had to spend the last two months in bed. 'Will you come?' she wrote, but I didn't want to venture among so many strangers, nor would Nadira have wanted me to go. Azizan died and she was not here, her child was born and I was not there.

Yet I felt as if I saw her often because I did, mostly late nights or early mornings, which used to be our times together, when the kothas grew quiet but we were still awake; now I'm always asleep or at least dozing at that hour. How many years do we spend in the world of dreams, and are there past, present, future in that world? Or does time move differently there? Most often, she appears as some version of her present self, travelling, running into me in an unknown location, preoccupied, polite, yet part of my quotidian existence. Occasionally, though, something memorable happens.

An unfamiliar courtyard. The morning of her wedding. Preparations all around. All of us, Ammi, Nadira, Azzo, Dadda, have moved into a large room and our bundles and boxes lie everywhere. Early morning, I find her in a room by herself, and ask if she wants some milk. She says yes, but it takes me time to find it and when I do, Dadda drinks it up. I'm looking for my clothes and can't find them but I find her, in a sari with flowers in her hair, looking miserable. She says she and the groom have quarrelled and are not talking, but it's all right because shaam tak gila ho jayega. I console her, stroking her hair, and am puzzling over whether gila can possibly mean something other than what it does mean. The men outside remark that the women will cry because that's what they always do at weddings. I find my trunk but the clothes in it don't seem to be mine. There's the groom's mother taking saris out of her box, and I find I'm beginning to cry.

~

I put down the pen and pick up the mirror. Without my noticing it, the hollow between my collar bones has filled in as my face has filled out, from a triangle becoming a doughy square. The body she touched is gone; someone else looks out of these eyes. Body and mind that are not me and not mine.

Now, nearly thirty years later, those two years seem complete with all the ups and downs of a lifetime, recalled at the moment of death. Only two Ramzans together, in smokeless, shuttered rooms, only two Diwalis, lighting the lamps on both rooftops, the insides of her translucent hands reddened by the steady glow in smoke-filled air. And numberless afternoons talking, musing, smoking, while both households slumbered.

Azzo began writing the last chapter when she went to Kashi twelve years ago, to train with Chapla for a couple of months. And returned two years later with baby Sona.

Kishen was married to a girl who spent most of her time in prayer and devotion. He and Azzo went with a troupe to Kalkatta, where Ganga meets the sea, and came back changed. Nadira was surprised but not displeased, and of course thrilled when it turned out to be a girl. After that, Chapla came more often, to see Sona. She had no daughter, after all. Kishen seemed less interested. Perhaps his wife disapproved.

Azzo brought back some poems. 'Look, Amma.' She bounced into my room, cheerful as always. Completely unlike the first Azizan. Full of energy and rarely despondent. Her questions are mostly the kind that need no answer. 'Chapla Mausi's poems. Kishen showed them to me and I copied the ones I like. Aren't they good? Sundar Apa says she would like to dance to this one. Oh, and I told Kishen that you and Mausi are friends. He didn't seem to know.'

No one from Banaras seems to know about any connection between her and me. 'How did you meet her?' a good friend of hers who was visiting once asked me, as if surprised I knew her. Why has she told no one? Because it doesn't matter any more? Because it matters too much? Am I betraying us by writing down our story? But no one will read it, and if they do, years hence, they won't know who we were.

Some of her poems I'd seen before, some I hadn't but still recognized. The sister-halves of poems I'd once written—mine seemed to rise beneath them like words written in milk when the paper heats up. Others were new, and I puzzled over them like the riddle-poems Mir Insha was fond of. Were they written to me or to others? Did they contain the answers to my questions?

Or were the answers buried in her eyes, smiling enigmatically at me over two feather-light heads, when she came to see little Sona? Rupa rarely came; she stayed in Kashi with Mohan.

Dadda's footsteps in the gallery, footsteps that used to interrupt us, heavier, more laboured now. She lumbers in. How old is she? Seventy? Eighty?

'Bitiya, Motilal Bhai is here. Bhajju wants you to help her choose fabrics.'

I slide my papers into the secret drawer of the writing-box our new Munshi-ji, the first one's younger brother, has procured for me, and make my way to Bhajju's room. Bhajju, dark, slender, and pushy from the time she was a toddler, is to become prince Nasiruddin's latest wife of sorts. He's married any number of women; and it's rumoured he will soon marry Sukh Chain, a slave at the palace, so this is not an important event. But because it's the first in our lane for at least ten years, something of a fuss is being made. Silks from Murshidabad, Hyderabad, Kashmir, Banaras, knee-deep on the floor. Bhajju's nursemaid holds them up against her and examines the effect critically, head on one side. Mughalani hovers in a proprietary manner, ready to interject. Motilal Bajaj, the older Motilal's son, leans back against a bolster and smiles proudly as he sips sharbat, careful to keep his black-and-white moustache out of it. But my mind is still with my papers and the fabric I see is that grey and yellow muslin sari she brought me from Kashi—'It's like sunlight on Ganga-ji at dawn,' she said. Lightest of muslins, *nainsukh*, joy of the eyes.

'Will Chapla bring her girls to dance if the English crown the Nawab a king?' The question comes out of nowhere, in that way Nadira has of getting inside my head.

'She hasn't yet decided. She may.'

'Yes, she often decides at the last minute, doesn't she?'

Now that the English have decided to crown the Nawab king for reasons of their own, Shirin will think herself a queen of some sort, though a junior and unofficial one. And Bhajju after she marries will consider herself a princess and a queen-in-waiting. If the coronation happens, it won't be for a year or two.

Sona comes in quietly and sits down, leaning against my knee. Her seven-year-old, even her five-year-old, self somewhere in her still, or is it her aunt I see? She has a face shaped like Azzo's, Kishen's nose and complexion but Chapla's eyes and mouth, at least so I think. She seems abstracted, fingering the cloth but thinking of something or someone else. How did Azzo, always sprightly, always full of laughter, produce this meditative child?

'Choose one for your birthday,' Nadira says, smiling at her, and I drape pink satin shot with blue over her shoulders. She slides it off. 'I don't want anything. I have too many clothes,' she says with the austerity of youth.

Nadira pulls a face at me, shaking her head. 'This child is like Sundar; she should have been born a *bhaktin*.'

'Like her father's wife,' Bhajju interjects pertly. Fortunately, Azzo is not in the room. Nadira's face is taut with anger, Sona gets up and leaves. I follow her. 'Don't let her bother you, bitiya, you know how she is.' I remember Madan advising me how to deal with Shirin's verbal weapons, as he pointed first to one side of his bald head and then the other, 'Take it in at one ear, let it pass through without touching anything, and let it out from the other ear.'

'It's not her. I just feel restless.'

'You want to go somewhere? Visit someone?'

'No, let's walk by the river.'

Not the place I'd have chosen in summer, but it turns out to be not as warm as I expected. The riverbank is quiet. A priest is performing rituals for a rustic couple on the steps. I smile, remembering Insha Sahib pretending to be a priest here and reciting *shloka*s for unwary villagers. We were surprised at how well he did it. He looked so good, his fair complexion set off by his white dhoti and the big red *tilak* on his broad forehead. Sona is not amused by the story. 'It's not right to deceive simple people.' She's right, though I wonder whether it was just a deception. I think it meant something to him. Three of his six pupils were Hindus; that is unusual.

'Chhoti Nani, look.' On the opposite bank, a troupe of jogin*s*. Supple, well-oiled bodies. A jogin for a day flashes before my eyes. And another one who threw a discus.

'Chhoti Nani, what was my grandfather like? Bari Nani never says much about him.'

I bite back my response, 'Because there's nothing much to say,' and dredge my memory for something positive. That he stuttered and had a fish-like stare doesn't seem appropriate.

'He was gentle and quiet. He used to come every single day to see her, for months, no, a couple of years.'

'Why didn't she stay on in Hyderabad?'

'She missed all of us, and his first wife didn't like her.'

If she had stayed she would have been a widow now, and your mother might not have met your father.

'Oh.'

She draws in the dust with her toe, still gazing across the river. Possibility haloes her face, curves her lips, droops her lashes. With a sudden change of mood, she jumps up. 'Let's go home. Ammi said she's making sweet rice tonight.'

On our way back, we pass the winding steps to Mattan Apa's kotha at the corner. I still think of it as Mattan Apa's but it belongs to all of us now. From the window pours Bakhshi's unchanged voice. Voices don't change as quickly as faces and bodies do. We had Ammi's fame to keep us going until we could groom our next star, and now we have Bakhshi's. Each kotha had about a dozen women then. Now that we have merged and expanded, and own three buildings that have become one, we have larger numbers, but none of the younger ones' voices yet matches Bakhshi's or so I think.

When we get back Motilal has left but now everyone is crowding around Hanuman, who's displaying jewellery. Everyone except Ammi, who sits gloomily in her shadow-filled room so I go to her and try to make small talk. She has put on weight, lost her litheness, but her eyes are the same—huge, thirsty, like the eyes of an imprisoned child.

I return to my room; Nadira has her own room now, next to mine. After so many years together, one needs some gaps, some spaces for quietude.

Madan comes in briefly to discuss the latest news, Wazir Ali's death. He was only thirty-seven. Madan is unusually agitated.

'The Company is behaving like a marauding wolf. First, they exiled Raja Chait Singh, your Chapla's father. He was a brave man and he fought back. And now this.'

I hesitate. 'Maybe I shouldn't say this now he's gone but, you must admit, he was somewhat crazy. Stabbing Cherry Sahib wasn't his first antic and it wouldn't have been his last.'

'All right, he was a bit crazy but I think the Company's insults made him crazier. First, they said he wasn't his father's son just because he was adopted, then they removed him after he had been enthroned, and put his old uncle in his place. And finally they locked him up in an iron cage in Kalkatta for seventeen years. Like a captured tiger for people to laugh and point at.'

'He was a maidservant's grandson. Our Nawab could have found someone better-born to adopt.'

'You and your ideas of high birth. He was raised as a prince. Remember how extravagant his wedding was? And he did manage to collect thousands to fight for him in Banaras after he had killed Cherry Sahib. Living in a cage and dying in a cage. Would have been better to kill him outright.'

To calm him down, I return to Raja Chait Singh. 'Did you know—after Raja Sahib finally gave up his fight against the Company and settled in Gwalior, he married Salamat, the dancer from Shahjahanabad?'

'What—the same one that foolish Ma'aruf, Miyan Rangin's pupil, was once so taken with?'

'The very same.' Ma'aruf who was also taken with our Azizan. What a mix—the people one has met, and the people one has heard of, all their garbled stories and entanglements jumbled up in one's head.

'That's too much. Everything connecting up neatly.' Madan laughs, then grows quiet. 'Well, he's gone now.'

'Yes, and so is Salamat. She died a year later.'

'And since then the Company keeps harassing the Maharajas in Kashi. Raja Udit Narayan has to put up with a lot, but he tries to fight back. And he's started the big Ramleela in Ramnagar. If the Company doesn't let him manage the affairs of the state, at least he has the people with him.'

'It's not as if the Companywallas don't harass our Nawabs. Perhaps there'll be another Raja Chait Singh fighting them soon, here or there or somewhere?'

'Or another Nawab Wazir Ali. Or someone who's a shadow of them. These days, everything seems to me like the shadow of something else.'

Bhajju's wedding does indeed appear like a shadow of earlier weddings. It's not that the colours have faded but that they appear less magical to me. Sharad still admires the young men's beauty but if I occasionally notice a woman it's one who's a faint echo of a memory.

I prefer my impossible fantasies—being asked to sing together, singing our song, Mir Rangin's ghazal about all things golden, and glimpsing recognition in her eyes. But when we meet, we are efficient, careful, generous, half-veiled.

She performs, grasped by all eyes, illuding all, and I watch. I see the resemblance to her mother that I couldn't see in our youth. Then she sits down in the front row, I'm in the back row. She turns her neck just a little, and something I thought long dead shoots through me.

I've been sitting at my desk for hours. My shoulder aches. As I'm about to doze off, Sona comes running in with the half-grown doe she has reared, Saloni the fourth, or is she the fifth? I slip my papers under an account book I keep ready for such interruptions.

'Look, Chhoti Nani, I've taught Sallo to stand on her hind legs.' She clicks her tongue and holds a fig above Saloni's head. Saloni rises up, her speckled coat rippling with eagerness.

'Sona, don't bring her upstairs - I've told you before.' Azzo comes in after her daughter. 'She's very badly behaved. She starts barking whenever Bhajju starts singing.'

Sona goes into peals of laughter. 'That's because Bhajju's voice is like a tiger's. It's good she's getting married; no one wants to hear her roar. You should hear Mitthu imitate her.'

'Nonsense.' Azzo bites back a smile. 'Go on, take her downstairs right away.'

'Come, Sallo, we're not wanted here.' The two of them prance off.

'Sonu,' I call after her. 'Ask if Mangu is back and if he's brought a letter.'

Azzo sits down and I stand up to stretch, Sona's laughter running through me like her aunt's so long ago.

'Bhajju and she are always after each other. I'm waiting for the wedding to be done with so we'll have some peace.'

'Bhajju is a little witch.' With age, my words have acquired sharp edges. 'Men may like that type but the prince's ladies will have their hands full.'

'Oh, I don't know about that. They may teach her a lesson. She'll be a daughter-in-law there, not a daughter.'

True, I think. Here, we are daughters forever.

~

I'm in a city looking for a place to stay. Someone tells me Chapla has found a place. I see everything in black and white, as I walk down an open gallery, until I open a door. The room is filled with light, with blazing colours. Someone is in the process of moving in— little tables, rugs, boxes, bottles, trays lie around. Madan is there, ready to take me to market to buy food, and Chapla is going with us. Then I discover that she's the one moving in here and so am I; all the preparations are ours, for us. I'm in a white dress with red sprigs on it of the kind the English ladies wear, and bright red shoes. I'm happy, so happy I could almost take wing, and I laugh aloud. We all drive off in Madan's horse carriage, she and I are discussing mundane matters, what we'll do later, how we'll arrange the rooms.

Things switch back to black and white, Madan and I are driving down a narrow street at night, and we lurch off the street, get into a minor accident.

There is more but it recedes as Sona calls from downstairs. 'He's back, Chhoti Nani. No letter for you.'

I wake briefly. I've been dozing in Nadira's room. Sharad has not replied.

Sharad's house, full of guests, clamour and confusion. After a while, he and I are walking down the lane towards home. The lane is like a village path running through fields, empty, dusty, lonely. He stops to buy sweets from a rustic. I check and find I have no money at all. We walk on and he casually says he has to return next day because he's decorating a new palace for the Nawab in his village. I'd expected him to stay several days. We reach our kotha, and it's locked. As I fumble for a key, he mutters something about being expected at the palace and takes off.

I'm startled awake. Never has a lock been seen on our door. Is it morning? No, it was a series of afternoon dozes, the distance between youth and old age.

Dadda comes in with a bundle of clothes. I sit up and rotate my shoulders.

'Can I give away these old things? You never wear them and there's a beggar girl outside asking for clothes.'

They are outfits I often wore in the years Chapla was here and then forgot all about. There's the red and black set Shirin discarded and I first wore to Mir Rangin's house, much too tight for either Shirin or me now. I feel a pang but say without looking through them, 'Yes, give them,' though I wonder what a beggar girl will do with such elaborate garments.

'She'll cut them up and sell the pieces,' Dadda explains, reading my dubious expression. Of course. Why do I often miss the obvious? She pads in again a while later and hands me a folded-up piece of old paper.

'This was in the pocket. Thought you might want it.' She looks at me, her face masked, as I open it gently, trying to avoid tearing it. For a moment my mind goes blank, then something submerged surfaces—it's a sketch of Chapla. The paper is worn along the seams.

Her youthful face, soft as the paper, creeps back into my brain. So small a face, a bud half-closed on the bough, such dark shadows under the watchful eyes. Her little body lost in the folds of the muslin sari wrapped round her. Bony expressive hands twisted before her as if in agony. This is Champa's sketch of her that she sent me after she had returned to Kashi that summer, the one I gazed at, kissed till my lips imbibed the lines, and lived on for three months. How could I not have missed it all this time? How could I have forgotten its existence?

And perhaps more important, how could I not have seen that she was terrified? Like a young deer startled out of hiding. What I had was a shadow, and this, that I hold, a shadow's shadow.

Memory, that most perfidious of hypocrites, holds up not a picture but a mirror. If she were telling the story, I realize, it would be almost entirely different from the one I recall.

Dadda remembered; she is one of the keepers of my secrets. She has her own secrets too. Heera told me one—as a girl of sixteen Dadda ran away from her village near

Delhi with a milkman. Both families disowned them, of course. They came to the city, where she found he already had a wife and two children. She was only twenty when he died, and his family blamed her. He used to deliver milk to my grandmother's kotha in Delhi, so Dadda found shelter there.

Heera appears in the doorway. 'Sharad Sahib is here to see you.'

'Really? It's that late?' He catches me straightening out my room.

'You're finally tidying up? Looks like you're doing it after years.' Age hasn't blunted his tongue but somehow what he says doesn't carry the sting it does when my mother says it. I smile and shake my head at him.

'You should get out and walk around, you know. Or open some windows. This room is musty. Reminds me of the parrot's cage. Look here.' He flicks some dust from a curtain.

'All curtains get dusty. Check them in your house and you'll see.'

'Mm.' He sits down and runs his fingers through his silver mane.

'Your hair looks nice. What have you done to it?'

'Jabakusum oil. Makes it shine.'

'How's everything? How are the dogs doing?'

'Very well.'

'Still biting everyone who visits?' My own tongue gets sharper in his company, I notice.

'Tch.' He waves an elegant hand. 'They don't bite anyone.'

'What are you saying? I saw Chand's leg after she visited you and what's his name—Kalu?—got hold of her.'

'Not Kalu, it was Manik. Moti only barks, he doesn't bite. And Manik bit her only because she got up to leave. He doesn't like anyone to leave the room. As long as you keep sitting he's perfectly happy. You come over and see. He's very friendly.' I'm exploding with laughter now but he's serious. 'Really. When Sona came he was so happy with her. He doesn't like boys. I think boys must have bothered him when he was young. And Chand looks like a boy sometimes.' His sweet smile appears as he says this. 'Where's Sona?'

'Around and about.'

'Is she healthy?'

'Yes, of course. Why?'

'Her father always looked unhealthy to me.'

'Kishen? As a child, do you mean? He wasn't unhealthy.'

'Hmm, I don't know. That's what I felt. Did you ever ask Chapla?'

'No.' Perhaps I had failed to see much that I should have seen. Could Kishen have been sickly and I not have noticed? Wouldn't she have said more about it?

Ammi looks in, nods to Sharu and asks when I'm next going to market. She hasn't got over the habit of disapproving of my unprofitable visitors, even though she's no longer in charge of finances or indeed anything else. Time, though, to draw the curtains, light the lamps, prepare for the long evening stretching into night.

Sharad leaves and Nadira comes in, holding a small bowl. 'How's that ache in your shoulder now?'

'Better, but still hurts.'

'Here, let me massage it.' She sits down and pours warm oil into one hollowed palm. The ache subsides and I almost fall asleep again as her practiced hands traverse the muscles.

A few weeks later, and Mangu has been returning empty-handed—no letter from Sharad though he did send mangoes from his orchards. He's caught up with neighbours, tenants, dogs, cousins, nephews and nieces. I'm on the roof but I can hear Ammi's voice at its harshest, berating Shabbo. Will I sound like that ten years from now? Do I already sound somewhat like that at times?

Sona comes into the yard and stands there, looking a little lost. As her aunt used to when she thought herself quite alone, she chews on her lower lip, her brow screwed up, but, then, like her aunt again, produces a dazzling smile as soon as Bakhshi's grandson comes to the backdoor to see if she wants to fly kites. Saloni follows them, stepping pointy-toed into the lane.

'Stop her,' I yell. 'The street dogs will get her.' Nadira pokes her head out from the kitchen. '*Arey*, calm down, the dogs are used to her. Sallo, come here.' She holds out a hibiscus flower and Saloni picks her way back across the yard.

I sit down to avoid observing what's going on below, but the rooftop is still hot so I have to stand up again, and I return to my room.

As I was writing this, Azzo came bounding in. Almost impossible to be alone, even for five minutes. 'Amma, Mir Rangin is here to see Ammi but she's gone with Nani to the dargah. He's crying. I don't know what to do.'

It was at least eight years since I'd seen him. I sprang up and went out to bring him in. He was crying indeed, and trembling. I made him sit down, fanned him, and told Shabbo to bring first iced water and then sharbat, watermelon, and the mangoes. Azzo and Sundar looked on with grave faces.

For a while he kept shaking his head in silence, then words poured out.

'I've just come to town and I went straight to see him, Nafis Bai. The door was hanging on its hinges—that door at which elephants used to sway! Ashurah Bhabhi came out, looking like a maidservant, and took me in. Nothing but dust and broken pots inside! He was sitting on the floor on an old straw mat. It was like a nightmare from which you can't wake up. He tried to put on a good show and welcome me. I'd been told he's not allowed to go out but he denied it. A little later, just to test the matter, I asked him to come with me and select a watermelon from the market. But he kept making excuses and trying to send the village urchin who's their only servant. Finally, he broke down and admitted it; the Nawab has forbidden him to step out of his house. He, who was the life of feasts and festivals! You've seen him, a freely blowing breeze—can he stay confined to those four walls? No more poems, no more jokes. It's all over, all over. We sat down and wept, that was the only thing left to do together.'

'But why?' I'd heard various rumours but hadn't seen Mir Insha for years. 'Is it because he made a foolish joke about the Nawab being the son of a maid? Or because he had gone to someone else's house on a day when the Nawab wanted him?'

'Maybe. Who's to say? More likely it was the manoeuvres of his false friends who envied him and betrayed him. Ma'aruf and company.'

So much had happened and his closest friend didn't know. How was it possible that two who were like a doubled orange flake, two halves of a walnut in a shell, could be broken apart—each alone in his own crowded house?

'His children's deaths destroyed him—first the boy and then the girl,' I said.

'What happened to her?'

'Maula'i Begam? She got cholera two years ago. And she had those two small children. Our Azzo had it too but she recovered.' Nadira and Sundar had nursed her through it. Sundar had sat day and night at Azzo's bedside, changing the wet cloths on her forehead, feeding her by hand.

'And Ta'ullah—what a beautiful boy he was, and so clever, just like his father. You remember how beautiful Mir Insha was?' I did. His iridescent scarves and shoes, always in the latest style. How he had shaved off his moustache and eyebrows to look like some of the azads, and how he preened before all of us, but then, later, when he happened to be alone with me, 'How do I look, Nafis Bai? Does it ruin my looks?' he had asked, turning so that I could see his profile.

'He was a fairy-faced one in his youth,' Rangin Sahib went on, repeating yet again what we had all heard many times. 'All Delhi's noblemen used to congregate to gaze at him when his father first brought him there; he was only fifteen. We've been friends since then, since boyhood. I can't imagine this city without him. Allah is the only truth, the rest are shadows.'

The moon is rising when he leaves. 'Chandni Khanam,' Mir Insha had named me, teasing, when he ran into me lingering late in the gallery by moonlight, waiting for her to slip over from next door. 'Ah, the light of the moon—it's meant for poets. No more poems, Nafis Bai?' I smiled, quietly exultant. 'The moonlight's enough for you now? But the poems will return when the moonlight vanishes.'

The poet is gone now, and so is the moonstruck girl.

9

'Has Kashi changed?' I ask one afternoon. We are in my new room that was once Shirin's, bigger, brighter than my two earlier ones. She sits near me, the residue of awkwardness now almost gone. Nadira and Rupa pop in and out, then go down to the children, whose laughter rises from the back alley.

'Well, people come and go. But not really. Queen Ahalya Bai and others have restored many destroyed temples so that's new. Your city has changed much more. So many more buildings.'

'Yes, and so many people gone. Mir Insha died two weeks ago.'

'No! What happened?'

'He'd been declining for a while. Last winter, Sharad told me that he suddenly showed up at a mehfil, looking decrepit and shabby, and sat down in a corner. At first, no one recognized him.'

'Shabby! He was always so exquisitely dressed.'

'Yes.' His grave look, when he told me I was fortunate. I am, in more than one way. 'Then he took a scrap of paper from his robe, and read that wonderful ghazal about the many departed friends and the few remaining ones. As he read, they guessed who he was, and the last verse made it clear, of course, but then he left quietly. And that's the last time he was seen.'

'How does it go?'

'I only remember the last couplet:

Kahaan gardish falak ki chain deti hai sunaa Insha
Ghanimat hai ki hum-surat yahan do chaar baithe hain
Listen, Insha, when do the revolving skies bring rest?
Fortunately, a few like-minded ones are gathered here.'

'That is wonderful. Say it again.' I did, and she repeated it softly. 'I wonder which departed friends he was thinking of. When did Miyan Jur'at go?'

'Was it six years ago, or seven? Around the same time as Almas Ali Sahib. What a eulogy Mir Insha wrote; that was one death he never quite got over.'

'Yes, Mir Insha thought the world of him.'

'Almas Ali deserved it until the end. Before he died, he threw into the tank all records of the debts people owed him. I wonder what became of his animals. He rescued so many, blind and lame ones too, Sharu told me, injured birds, abandoned cows and horses, crippled deer. Sharu liked to go there to get away from court intrigues and relax among the animals.'

A pause, then I said, 'Look, when Mir Rangin came by last, he gave me this.' I lifted the book from its wrappings. 'It's his rekhti volume. He said so much of it was based on what all of us had told him or told Mir Insha or Sharad that I should have a copy. I keep it with my copy of *Darya-e Latafat*.'

'Ah, the one Rangin Sahib and you helped with.'

'Yes, ever so many years ago. Time seems to pass faster now than it did earlier – do you find that?'

'Yes, why is it?'

'A spool unwinds faster as you near the end.'

She sat reading a few poems to herself, while I looked at her, wondering, as I often do after meeting her, whether I've been talking too much. Yet, when she looked up, I couldn't stop myself from showing her the picture she had sent me long ago—two women on a rooftop under the moon. 'Remember this?'

She looked at it, her face blank, and said nothing.

So I was not the only one who had forgotten details? I was disappointed but should I have been relieved? Was it possible she was pretending not to remember? Because it was unimportant? Or too important? Or embarrassing? Was the girl I once adored gone for ever? This was a book I would never be able to stop reading because I would never fully understand it.

~

'Couldn't sleep much today,' Nadira says. We're in my room, and she's copying out a poem.

'It happens to all of us as we grow older. Don't worry about it, just sleep when you can.'

'Not worrying. But if I get up and read my mind wakes up and that's it. If I keep lying awake I get restless.'

'Hmm, I know. I think being always surrounded by chatter keeps one's brain awake. Leave the mehfil early tonight and spend some time on your own before bed. I'll manage things there. How are your knees?'

'The same. I should shed some weight. Oh, I forgot to tell you—Heera and her children are going to her husband's village for two months. Next week.'

'It's not the best time. Dulari is with her parents too. And Mahtab Baji needs her special diet. But Shabbo is here.'

'She's not much of a cook. Maybe Heera can teach her a few things before she leaves.'

We continue chatting intermittently. An unmatched comfort, these sleepy afternoons together.

'I'd better go and have a bath.'

'All right. I'll see if Azzo and Sundar have any ideas about finding us a cook for two months.'

She collects her papers and stands up slowly, holding on to a table.

I'm bathing when the screaming and crying starts. That's not unusual in a house where so many women live together, but it has an ominous undertone this time. I hurry to finish, and follow the sounds to Azzo's room.

As I enter, Nadira puts her head on my shoulder and weeps. Azzo is quiet as if stunned. Sundar has an arm round her and the other round Sona. Two days ago, Kishen was out in the heat all day, buying goods at the wholesale market in Kashi for his little grocery shop in their alley. He collapsed and died before they could get him home or to a doctor. The news has just reached us.

To me he's still the child sometimes old beyond his years; I've only seen him a couple of times since then. *When my mother dies, I'll stand in front of a carriage.* He has outrun her in the race every mother wants to win.

When Chapla next visits, she looks older for the first time ever. They had known, she says, ever since he was a baby, that he was likely to die young. All kinds of doctors had examined his pulse and said he had a weak heart; an astrologer had predicted it too. This was the shadow that had followed her and of which she had never spoken. To speak of it would have been inauspicious, would have endowed the shadow with form and features. But in the silence grew many other shadows. Ketaki Mausi is distraught. She has Mohan to comfort her, a sort of reflection of Kishen. I've often noticed it—although among us, girls are the desired children, not boys, and in the world outside it's the other way round, yet the undesired children are usually cherished just as much.

Now all four of us talk as those talk who have walked through a tunnel and come out on the other side, into a world of endings. She's sitting next to me, unconscious of herself as she tells us about him.

There are different kinds of *bekhudi*. I see as if for the first time the face still precious to me—ordinary in its extraordinariness. Lightning that rarely strikes twice. Not a dream. Not the past but this moment.

'Chapla's here?' Madan asks when he visits that evening, and I realize that her name produces no tremor. Under the skin, now not like a fragment of glass vexing and vexed, but like blood in my veins, composed of many elements. Both of us and neither of us, circulating in the stream of things while we watch.

Next day, she says, 'Azzo, Sundar and Sona are coming to Kashi next month, and maybe Nadira too. Will you come?'

'Yes, I'll come.'

I'll stand on the shore of that river which bears all things away and brings them back changed yet the same.

Historical characters

Poets

Insha Allah Khan 'Insha': 1756–1817.
Sa'adat Yar Khan 'Rangin': 1755–1835.
Shaikh Qalandar Bakhsh 'Jur'at': 1748–1810.
Wali Mohammad 'Nazir Akbarabadi': 1735–1830.
Ghulam Hamdani 'Mushafi': 1751–1824.
Hazrat Khwaja Hasan, friend of Jur'at, dates unknown.

Rulers and Nobility

Asaf-ud Daula ruled Awadh: 1775–1797.
Wazir Ali ruled Awadh: 1797–98.
Sa'adat Ali Khan ruled Awadh: 1798–1814.
Ghaziuddin Haider Shah ruled Awadh: 1814–1827; crowned by the British in 1818.
Raja Chait Singh ruled Banaras: 1770–1781.
Maharaja Udit Narayan Singh ruled Banaras: 1795–1835.
Almas Ali Khan: died 1808.
Raja Tikait Rai: 1760–1808.

Europeans

George III: born 4 June 1738.
Sophia Plowden: in India 1777–1790.
Claude Martin (companion Gori Bibi): in India 1751–1800.
Antoine Polier (Indian wives Jugnu and Zeenat): in India 1757–1788.
Johan Zoffany: in India 1783-89.
Benoit de Boigne (first wife Noor was converted and renamed Helene): in India 1778–1796.
John Mordaunt: died 1790, aged about forty.

Tawaifs

In his poem on King George the Third's fiftieth birthday celebrations, Insha describes Chapla Bai dancing, and he also wrote a poem about Dulhan Jaan's marriage. Rangin wrote a verse epistle to Farkhanda tawaif. Jur'at's masnavi recounts the romance of Hazrat Khwaja Hasan and Bakhshi Tawaif, and he also wrote a chronogram for the death of Azizan tawaif. Munshi Tota Ram's *Tilism-e Hind* narrates the incident about Sundar tawaif, the Nawab and the *dastan-go* from Pratapgarh. We know nothing more about these characters.

Acknowledgements

'It is a very strange feeling,' remarked Gertrude Stein, '. . . when you write a book and while you write it you are ashamed for . . . you know you will be laughed at or pitied by every one and . . . you are not very certain and you go on writing. Then some one says yes to it . . . and then never again can you have completely such a feeling of being afraid and ashamed . . .'

I am grateful to Sujata Raghubir who was the first to say yes to it, to Mona Bachmann for reading an early draft and discussing title options, to Katherine O'Donnell for her crucial comments on a mid-way draft, and to Geetanjali Shree for reading a late draft and making useful suggestions. Thanks to Sanju Mahale, Ravi Mehta, Leela Gandhi, Siddhartha Gautam, Masooma Ali, and my son, Arjun, for various kinds of inspiration, and to my grandmother, Victoria Nirmalini Desai *nee* Mukherjee, for the incident of the clothes copied by neighbours, which occurred during her childhood in Bareilly. Many thanks to Richa Burman, my editor at Penguin, for her efficiency, helpful suggestions, and support.

All translations of Urdu poems are by me, from manuscripts in the Raza library, Rampur. Several episodes narrated by the poets derive from their prose and verse writings.

As always, special thanks to Mona and Arjun.